Forest of the Dead: Stories of Transformation

Diane Wing

Published by Vibrant Concepts Publishing, 2024.

This is a work of fiction. Similarities to real people, places, or events are entirely coincidental.

FOREST OF THE DEAD: STORIES OF TRANSFORMATION

First edition. April 6, 2024.

ISBN: 979-8223681526

Written by Diane Wing.

Table of Contents

For the brave souls who embark on their own transformative journeys.

Praise for Forest of the Dead: Stories of Transformation

"I want more!!!!!!!!!!!!! I loved every story." — Fern Granoff, Plymouth Meeting, PA

"EACH STORY PROMPTS the urge to reflect and journal. A good book will resonate and provide an ah-ha moment, a reminder of what is known but forgotten. This is that book. It touched a rainbow of senses, a spectrum of memories dark and pleasant, logic and reason, quirkiness, mysticism, spirituality, elementary common sense, and left me with a thirst for more. Will there be a sequel or a movie?"

— Annette Sadelson, Baltimore, MD

"WHAT A JOY THIS BOOK is! It's the spiritual journey of Samuel, a 38-year-old man whose mother has died recently. She arranged to be buried in Willow Ponds Cemetery or, as locals called it, The Forest of the Dead. Samuel doesn't understand why his mother wanted to be buried in what he considers to be a creepy place. Worse, in order to be close enough to visit on a regular basis, he has to sell his comfortable home and relocate to a strange town where he knows no one. However, on each visit to the cemetery, he encounters spirits who live in the trees, and each spirit tells a story about its life. Through these stories, Samuel becomes more aware of the mystical world around him. I loved all the tree spirits' stories. The novel grabbed me right away and kept me captivated to the very end. I highly recommend this book!!" — Terri Chalmers, Sicklerville, NJ

"I just finished your book and wow! It was intriguing, enveloping, inspiring, and soul transmuting. I saw so much of me throughout the book in odd ways that I can't describe. It's such a beautiful book about the trees and their stories. As I went into the story of Charlotte, I began crying. I don't know why. The fulfilling story of the forest magic delighted me.

"I couldn't stop the sense of intrigue and beauty of the many psychic gifts others have and how they impact humanity in such beautiful ways, shifting the world in subtle, soulful ways. It was just magical how you weaved yourself, your wisdom, and the characters into a potent instruction of how to find ourselves through transformation. It was a book filled with spiritual inspiration and magic that I will allow to wash me into my rebirth this spring."

— Lyn Hicks, Longmont, CO, author of *The Lotus Project: The Art of Being a Woman*

"EVERY EVENING, WHEN I rejoined Samuel's journey, I was transported through the Forest of the Dead. And, each time I was forced to close the pages at night, I found myself thinking and seeing my life differently. There is magic in our natural world and the stories of the people around us. I now believe that, like Samuel, my "view of the world has shifted." I wouldn't have thought it possible that so much was awakened. I'm in awe of what I discovered in such a short book!"

— Nila Sinha, Ph.D., Dallas, TX

"MOST BOOKS ARE SIMPLY books, delivering stories to readers eager to escape into formulaic relief from everyday life. *The Forest of the Dead - Stories of Transformation* is not one of those. The tales within this book are told by the spirits residing within the magical trees in Willow Ponds Cemetery, a mysterious, secluded forest that is the final resting place of unique individuals deemed worthy of spending eternity with their chosen trees.

"Travel with Samuel on his enlightening journey. Experience the wisdom of the trees. Willow Ponds may be the place you choose to spend your eternity - but are you qualified to rest there?

"Diane Wing's endlessly fascinating imagination, scholarly knowledge, and deep originality shine in her latest literary offering. Enter Wing's Forest of the Dead and discover what truths await you!" — Maxine Ashcraft, Oakland, CA

Books by Diane Wing...

Cozy Mysteries with Chrissy the Shih Tzu

Attorney-at-Paw

The Dog-Eared Diary

Trick-or-Doggy Treat

A Winter's Tail

Housebroken Honeymoon

Dark Fantasy

Coven: The Scrolls of the Four Winds

Thorne Manor and other bizarre tales

Trips to the Edge

Non-fiction

The True Nature of Tarot: Your Path to Personal

Empowerment, 10th Anniversary Edition

The True Nature of Energy: Transforming Anxiety into Tranquility

The Happiness Perspective: Seeing Your Life Differently

Acknowledgements

I am deeply grateful to those who took the first journey into the stories I've shared in these pages. To my beta readers, Maxine Ashcraft, Terri Chalmers, Fern Granoff, Lyn Hicks, Annette Sadelson, and Nila Sinha, my deepest gratitude for your honesty and encouragement.

To my editor and friend, Terri "Eagle Eye" Chalmers, for her work to make this book sparkle.

Those who inspire me hold a special place in my heart and my work. My deepest thanks to Caroline Kranick for being the inspiration for *The Tattoo Artist* story.

Special thanks to author Santosh Kalwar for permission to use his insightful quote about trees.

A very special shout-out to my dear friend, tireless reader, and courageous soul who shares her thoughts about my work honestly and unflinchingly, Maxine Ashcraft. I treasure our connection, the effortless cognitive alignment we share, the laughter, your endless patience, and your devotion to polishing this manuscript beyond what I could do alone.

And to my readers, who motivate me to keep creating and innovating, much love.

Notes

This book was professionally edited and proofread. However, if you encounter any typos or formatting issues, please contact me at diane@dianewingauthor.com so we can correct it. Thank you.

The intentional spelling of magick with a "k" differentiates the illusion of the magician (magic with a "c") from the magick within you, wherein you have the freedom to be yourself, use your gifts, and serve those you care about in extraordinary ways.

“All our wisdom is stored in the trees.”

— Santosh Kalwar

Samuel's Journey Begins

Samuel Jones walked through the ancient, eerie forest for the second time since he planted his mother here last month. The funeral home's limousine brought him to the cemetery for the first time. Attendees included himself, the funeral director, and a stranger who carried a shovel and dug the hole for his mother's tree. No one prayed over her grave; only his silent goodbye. There were no cars in the small visitor's parking lot and no visitors to other graves.

Hundreds of crows filled the trees as they did the day his mother, Charlotte, died from pneumonia. He wondered what she was thinking when she wrote her last wishes with the aid of an attorney. By the day of her death, she was tired of living and grappling with whatever demons opened emotional wounds that had never healed.

Charlotte pre-paid for her natural burial with the funeral home and specified her ashes become resident in Willow Ponds Cemetery, otherwise her son would not have done it. Samuel preferred the more formal, sterile environment of a vault within a mausoleum closer to their family home rather than visiting his mother in the dark, dense forest that felt alive with people, although none were visibly present. No other visitor picked their way down the unkempt dirt trails to access the tree of their loved one.

Charlotte taught Samuel the spiritual meanings of the trees from when he was a child. They'd hike through parks, naming trees and discussing their attributes. Charlotte Jones chose the sturdy trunk and broad leaves of a sycamore to house her soul. Research told Samuel it was the tree of gifts and support, a role she played in life with friends, family members, and strangers. Its intricate root system represented the stability of gaining wisdom to navigate life's challenges, which fit Charlotte's life philosophy. In some cultures, the sycamore symbolized the power of seeking spiritual enlightenment and the potential for personal transformation.

Her choice puzzled him, despite their excursions to the park. In all the hours they spent before and during her illness, she never mentioned this type of burial prior to her death. He assumed she'd want to be buried in a shiny wood casket and preserved in a vault. Unaware that his mother had a proclivity toward environmental burials, he was angry that she never shared this with him. Now, heavy with her loss, he couldn't find out more about her decision. She had kept an entire part of herself hidden from him. Why would she want to spend eternity in these creepy woods?

Known to the locals as the Forest of the Dead, its occupants were cremains planted in an urn containing the decedent's choice of a tree sapling. Many of these massive trees were likely two hundred years old or more. He could not tell which ones were planted in the name of the deceased and which might have simply sprouted up on their own.

Charlotte's final resting place was in a remote part of Pennsylvania. Samuel needed to sell the home he grew up in and move within an hour of the cemetery in order to visit his mother as stipulated in the will. She left him shockingly well off. He never had to hold a regular job again. Good thing, too, since there were not businesses nearby to acquire gainful employment. Her instructions required him to study the forest she had chosen for herself and, ultimately, wanted him planted in, as well.

There was no definitive history of these woods or when it became a cemetery. Rumors swirled about that it used to be an Indian burial ground possessing supernatural qualities that hastened tree growth. Questioning the funeral director, Samuel discovered that an occult society, their purpose shrouded in mystery, determined who could have eternal rest at Willow Ponds. When Samuel pushed him further, there was no other information available. There was a phone number given only to funeral directors and members of the society to call when a request came to become part of the forest. The person at the other end of the line either gave permission or didn't. Ninety percent of the time, they allowed the planting. When they didn't, they gave no reason. No one knew the name of the society or of the person who answered the phone. An internet search proved futile. How his mother found out about this place was beyond him.

With five hundred acres filled with trees fueled by the ashes of the dead mixed with rotting leaves, the smells and mist gave the place a spooky vibe. Even in the newly planted area where Charlotte's remains rested, the sense of intelligent energy permeated the field of young trees. The sycamore grew two feet over the last couple of weeks, its expected growth rate for a year, the cemetery soil giving it the strength to force its branches to spread. His mother's energy reached out to him from the fast-growing sapling she had become since being planted a couple of months prior.

Samuel usually took the gravel path from the black wrought-iron gates directly to his mother's resting place, but despite this muggy August day, the recent rain made the trees supple and bright. The freshness of the rain mingled with the scent of decay. Samuel's feet disappeared into the twilight mist rolling across the trail. This part of the forest hummed as though the tree roots vibrated along the ground, calling to him. He shivered in the August heat as he witnessed the trees quivering without the aid of wind.

He followed the trail to an oak grove, with one of the oak trees stretching fifty feet, vying for the sunlight in the densely wooded cemetery. Beyond was a pond overhung by a circle of massive weeping willows. A thirty-foot tall oak stood out, with a large hollow in its trunk. Samuel wondered if a creature lived inside. He cautiously approached, wary of something flying out or jumping from the hole. Instead, in the soft light of evening, a radiance beckoned him to investigate.

He cautiously made his way toward the majestic oak tree, his foot sinking into a pile of wet leaves. Moisture leaked into his sneaker. Disgusted by mud and decaying water coating his formerly white athletic sock, Samuel shook out his shoe and tread more carefully to avoid soaking his other foot.

A few more feet, and he was eye-level with the glowing oval cavity. It measured about a foot high and half as wide. The illumination came from the base of the opening and looked similar to embers from a dense fire. He reached palm down into the space, but no heat emanated from the brightness. Instead, a sigh came from the hole, along with a whoosh of air. A scroll appeared; its text written on oddly wrinkled paper. As Samuel unrolled the parchment, a vision flashed in his mind. This wasn't made of animal hide, but rather human skin. Repulsed, he dropped it on the ground.

A moan floated from the tree. *This was my flesh. These are my secrets.* Apparently, it wanted Samuel to pick up the scroll; he did so reluctantly. The light pulsed and instructed him to sit on the rock behind him while he read.

Samuel brushed debris from the stone and sat. It formed a natural seat, smooth, as though many had sat in this spot to read this story. It was the tale of the person whose ashes were part of this oak tree. He remembered his mother's metaphysical lessons about trees and knew that oak stood for strength and power. It could also open doorways to inner realms. As he read, Samuel realized how true to character the deceased's choice of tree was.

The Mage
Oak: Power & Strength

In 1938, I, Arthur Mayfair, was a boy living in the Pocono Mountains of Pennsylvania. We had a two-bedroom cabin. My father did odd jobs around the area and my mother grew vegetables and flowers to sell by the road.

The locals said Ma's produce filled them with energy. When they placed her flowers in their homes, they had the desire to be kinder to all who entered. Pa had a reputation for fixing any household problem, from leaks in the roof to mechanical failures in the boiler. He once told me he apprenticed with his dad, who taught him how to *listen* for the damaged item to speak and tell him how to restore it.

Folks stared at me as I rode my bike through town or when I was at school. One time, I asked someone in my grade why he was looking at me. The kid said they were waiting to see what powers I had. I told him I didn't have any. I remember he said, "Just you wait."

So, I waited. I asked Ma about it. She said, "Your special gifts will come out when it's time."

I figured she was right, since she was rarely wrong about me. Many times, she reached inside of me and pull out the exact information I needed to know. Maybe all mothers could do that, but I only knew about mine.

One day, I was sitting in my third-grade classroom as usual. Everyone sat face forward, listening to the teacher give a history lesson, when a shot of *knowing* hit me in the center of my forehead and then moved to my heart. I gasped, loud enough for the kids on either side of me to turn and look as I clutched my chest. Where had it come from? I scanned the room and saw a glow around a girl in the front row.

My senses homed in on her until another shot came. This time, I was ready for it. Total sadness overwhelmed me, matching her level of sorrow. After class, I ran up to her and asked if she was all right. She shared that her dog had died the night before. He was her best friend. I never had a pet, but imagined what it would be like to lose a friend if I had one.

I touched her shoulder in support. My heart lifted, and yellow light came out of my hand and into her, reaching her chest where the most pain was. She sighed, looked at me, and thanked me for talking to her. Her mood was better, having told me what was wrong. As she walked away, her glow was brighter. Most of the darkness had left.

That's when I realized my gift had finally come! I could make people feel better. But did it work both ways? Could I make people feel bad? Did I have to touch them to make it happen?

I kept my newfound gift to myself, testing it with lots of locals of all ages, male and female, even animals. People glowed with different colors, sizes, and intensities. I learned which ones reflected loneliness, which was depression, and which was love. When people loved another person, their shine got bigger and brighter. Ma and Pa had that kind of glow when they were near each other. If someone didn't like another person, their aura turned dark and spikes of energy were directed toward the enemy.

After observing someone, I'd talk to them and see how they were doing. It came across as polite, casual conversation. I didn't take action on these observations and kept my gift a secret, even from my parents. As a kid, I wasn't sure what to do with them. I kept track of what I saw in the back of my notebook. The right time would come; it just wasn't right now.

One day, as I sat observing passersby, I saw a different kind of glow. It wasn't all the way around the person, but rather a single dark spot in their lower torso. This spot was more physical and less emotional. The rest of him hummed with the dim light of sadness. When the man sat on a bench across from me, I walked over and struck up a conversation with him. Turned out he had liver cancer and didn't have much longer to live. When he bowed his head, I sensed his grief. Grabbing his hand, I sent a stream of energy into him, picturing the dark spot filling with white light. He lifted his head, eyes opened wide, and beamed a smile at me. The sad hum was gone and so was the dark spot. I smiled back and told him to have a good day.

That's when the rumors started. But I guess if the story is true, it's not really a rumor. Now when I walked through town, people stared and whispered. Word got back to Ma and Pa. They wanted to hear more about my gift and why I hadn't shared it with them. Not knowing what it was or what to do with it was my excuse. There wasn't any reason to keep my parents in the dark, so I spilled my experiences and observations to them over dinner, including the encounter that spurred the rumor mill. They listened intently as they ate, waited until I finished, and then each took my hand.

They told me the story about my family back generations on both sides. They married to make sure their child had a gift that could help humanity, and the importance of telling them before using my gift to ensure it was what they called *the highest good*. I wasn't sure what that meant, but I trusted them.

As word spread about a healer living in the town, people came to the house regularly looking for me to heal their physical and emotional pain and ailments. Ma explained that simply taking away their problems harmed them in other ways. Spirit gave them their circumstances to teach them about life. If I got rid of it, I also removed the lesson. I grew to understand this idea as I got older, but those who came to me did not.

I did what I could and cleared the unwanted glow from lots of folks. My desire to make people happy was my intention all along, thinking that people would smile and be grateful. Yet, they focused on the times I turned someone away; the locals threatened to punish me if I didn't use my gift. The community judged me and my family, saying we were selfish and refused to help because we wanted more money. Actually, we wanted to help, but with guidance from Spirit's will. We tried to explain this to them. We even went to the minister of the church so he could help them understand about Divine Will, to no avail.

One night, after turning away a man who had cheated on his wife and came down with a venereal disease, he and his friends came to our cabin carrying clubs and threatening to burn our house down. Pa went outside to talk sense to them while Ma held me close inside the house. We heard the men yelling and Pa saying that illness that came from sin was not to be healed with his son's gifts. That I would lose my ability to heal anyone else if I did so. This seemed to lessen their wrath. I guess Pa got them thinking about all the others who would lose out if their friend, whose illness was his own fault, received healing.

It got me thinking, too, about the danger my gift put me and my family in. So, after the men left, Ma, Pa, and I packed up our meager belongings, picked the food and flowers from Ma's garden, and left town in our pickup truck. We moved far enough that no one knew who we were or what we could do for them. That's how my family and I became nomad mages, so that we could help others for a time and then move on before the townsfolk would demand we use our gifts as they saw fit and jeopardize our very existence.

Samuel's Unfolding Awareness

Samuel sat back, feeling as though he had watched the story play out rather than reading it. He saw every interaction, experienced the heart-pounding confrontation and escape of Arthur Mayfair and his family, and again wondered why his mother would want to spend eternity in this forest. He shook his head to bring himself back to the present. Slowly rolling up the scroll, the trance still upon him, he placed it back into the knot of Mayfair's oak and watched it disappear and the light go out before heading out of the cemetery.

The trees took on a new meaning for him as he made his way down the path and through the gate. Strange birdsong and insect sounds filled the woods and beckoned him back the following day. Samuel's mind couldn't escape from the secrets he had yet to uncover and ultimately determine the mystery of his mother's burial request. Could it be her desire for him to experience the stories held within the trees? How had she known that he would need to visit often for him to get a full understanding of those buried here?

He returned the next day and walked toward the pond surrounded by graceful willows. Samuel had spent the previous night studying his mother's books about the energies of trees and discovered that willow represented intuition, dreams, divination, magick, and death. He wondered what messages the willows would bestow upon him and whether he was ready to hear them.

One tree looked brighter than the rest, so he made his way over to it. He placed his hand gently on the trunk and watched a portal open, this time containing a small book. He reached into the portal with less trepidation than with the oak and lifted the book from its nest. The cover, made of multicolored, iridescent silk, was smooth on his palm. He hoped the story it contained was calmer than the first. A folding chair appeared behind him, so he made himself comfortable and began to read.

The Psychic
Willow: Divination & Death

I, Sabina Lovell, was famous for my psychic powers. Known under my professional name, Persephone, my gifts emerged at seven years old. Mom gave me the name to protect our identity.

With family finances strained after my father left, my mother exploited my talents to those who could pay for my counsel. She excelled at finding those in need and speaking highly of my abilities. We made a decent living with my psychic sessions, and she contributed to our income by providing erotic services while I was in school. She denied it, but the men's passions lingered in our home, and I was revolted by some of their sick fantasies.

As a teenager, I spent time in the metaphysical bookstore down the street to find information about protecting myself from unwanted energies and employed these practices before each of my sessions. I saged the couch I slept on and stayed out of my mother's bedroom.

In Los Angeles in the 1960s, people were open to having information come through from the other side. Where it came from, I don't exactly know, but it was accurate. Even as a child, I simply channeled the information, most of which I didn't understand. I spoke as it came through and rarely remembered my visions or what I said. Word spread, and soon I was reading for the wealthy and the famous. In private social circles, those who required reassurance, information about investments, and guidance about love relationships whispered my name and regularly came to our one-bedroom apartment to receive guidance.

My influence became absolute with those who sought my services. They trusted Mother and me not to reveal personal information about them or their sessions, especially the married men who purchased additional services from my mother.

As the years passed, my interests extended beyond the affairs of others. I sought a social life among the few teenage friends I made at school while doing normal things for my age group, like going to the mall and the movies. My stage name, as I called it, allowed me to keep my gifts secret from them. Their criticism of characters in the movies who had psychic ability showed how afraid they were of someone who could reveal their deepest secrets. And I could. All it took was touching a piece of their jewelry to know what they did when they were alone or how insecure they were despite projecting confidence. Those I spent time with had the most innocuous habits and beliefs, otherwise the strain would be too great. My work exposed me to the swampy excesses and fears of people; I didn't want to deal with it among my friends.

When I turned 18, I saw my mother's aura go dull and knew a sexually transmitted disease would take her from the physical realm. I moved from my mother's apartment after she transitioned and got a place of my own. The entrance off the street led to a parlor where I set up a cozy reading room filled with candles, crystals, comfortable seating, a small glass table for individual readings, and a large wooden table that could accommodate a group. I reserved the upstairs as my living quarters, giving me something I'd always longed for but never had—privacy and separation from the energies of others.

The regular customers I started with as a child fell away from my practice because of age, illness, or disinterest. There was no need to advertise. People in the community still recognized the name Persephone, and they sent referrals to my new location.

My talents grew and expanded to mediumship. Before, I could read the auras of people and get images from the items they brought me, and now I started seeing their deceased loved ones. I didn't always tell them, for many times, it was an omen of the client's death rather than a loving message from the other side. Sometimes the dead that followed them into my parlor weren't loved ones at all. Sometimes the dead came to accuse the client of something they did to the person when they were alive. I could see the entity walk in with the client; its energy ever present. The heaviness that the client experienced was likely from their invisible companion, undermining them every step of the way.

When I left my house, the issues people were dealing with surrounded me; I picked up on the impressions left by those who touched produce and boxes at the grocery store, and watched the deceased follow those they were connected to in life. I tried sensing my mother, but her spirit was not with me. I kept my living quarters physically and spiritually clean. It was the only place I got a break from the constant bombardment of other people's issues, both living and dead.

My telepathic interactions with the dead taught me many things about people, from their fears to their aspirations and what they hated and loved. Those who stepped foot in my salon had experienced trauma, suffered from a fear of the future, or carried worry that the past was catching up with them. The constant exposure to these feelings wore me down, despite the wards and shields I employed.

I learned how to best impart the information that released the client and their shadow if the client took my advice. It gave me some relief, as well as the client, to lighten their load. About eighty percent listened to me; the other twenty percent denied my reading and left as unhappy as they were before entering my parlor.

One day, I was making tea in the kitchen when the bell over the entry door tinkled. I came into the parlor and stopped short. A young man stood in the center of the room. Next to him was my mother! He looked at her, and then at me, commenting that I was the spitting image of my mother. Astonished that he could see her, I fell into my high-back chair, unable to speak. I reached out to my mother with my thoughts and asked why she was here and with this man.

He was the son of the man who caused her death. The man nodded as though he could hear her response and plunked a cloth bag with leather handles onto the table. It looked expensive. He informed me that his father had been in love with my mother. It was unintentional that he exposed my mother to the fatal illness that took her from me and that also caused his own death. In the bag was his apology and recompense.

I unzipped the bag and found mounds of banded bills in denominations of hundreds and twenties. My mouth dropped open. I stuttered, trying to find the words. He held up his hand and assured me that this is what his father wanted and also that my mother wanted to free me from the life she thrust me into.

Another spirit entered the room and stood next to my mother, smiling. The young man nodded and waved goodbye while the spirits of my mother and her lover gradually faded. So much love was in the room that it took my breath away. I looked again at the contents of the bag and an image flashed into my mind as it did in readings I did for others. A small, beautiful cottage surrounded by a picket fence, nestled in the country. A dog happily playing in the yard. It was where I lived out my days and finally found peace and freedom from the negativity that plagues humanity.

Samuel's Clarity of Vision

Samuel smiled as the story concluded, happy that Sabina finally found the life she deserved. It must have been difficult to deal with the problems of others every day all day long. Sabina's insights into people must have been disturbing. He couldn't imagine a life such as she lived. He rose from the folding chair, and it disappeared. Samuel placed the book gently back into its portal and watched it dissolve.

The woods became silent. A sense of dread ensued. Movement caught his eye. A hooded figure floated through the dense growth. Was this, finally, another human visiting their loved one? Doubt consumed him as fear dampened the beat of his heart. The person stopped and looked. No face was beneath the hood. It may be a trick of light and shadow or the distance between Samuel and the figure. Maybe. Until the form suddenly vanished. Samuel understood nothing was as it seemed in these woods, in this Forest of the Dead. An urgent need for light overcame him. He needed to find an open, bright spot in the dense woods.

Samuel scanned the area and found sunlight beaming down onto a meadow. He made his way toward it, huffing and puffing, pressing to get away from the dim area where the hooded figure dwelled. A hazel tree stood alone, bathed in light, the sun nurturing every leaf. Samuel wanted the sun to cleanse his apprehension and hastily made his way to the tree.

A few hazelnuts poked their shells from beneath the leaves. Samuel's stomach rumbled, but also jellied from fright. He'd wait a few minutes before trying one of the nuts the tree offered. The hazel branches grew low, so sitting beneath it was out of the question, instead, making himself comfortable on the grass beside it. He rested, caught his breath while looking around to make sure whatever was in the woods had not followed him, and then reached up and plucked a nut from the tree.

Upon doing so, a scroll dropped out of the tree. Samuel couldn't see where it fell from. Tied with a red ribbon that he slid off of the document, he unrolled it and jumped into the story.

The Teacher
Hazel: Wisdom & Inspiration

The idea of standardized tests appalled me. As a teacher of thirty years' experience, I, Andy Bartholemew, knew no test could measure the potential of a child or, for that matter, an adult. Many adults still sought their purpose and their gifts. That's what my job was: to discern what a student's innate special talent was. I realized my own abilities when I started seeing people as having a particular quality about them. My keen sense of people tracked into their ultimate vocation. Most times, I saw the brightness in them. Other times, it was apparent that the person held darkness within and would likely end up incarcerated or functioning on the darker side of life.

When the administration announced class assignments, kids and parents hoped to get into my courses. The kids wanted to find out what they would become, and the parents wanted to avoid paying college tuition if their child was not of the caliber for higher education. The funny thing was that I taught English, not a reach-your-potential class.

Together, the school administration and I figured out that it wasn't until a student was at least 11 years old before I could work my magick and impart my wisdom as to their future. But there was still room for change. Free will, after all, is still active with any prediction, regardless of what potential I see. The possibilities might expand or contract, depending on the cooperation and interests of the student and their guardians.

Some parents refused to believe it when the signs indicated their child's opportunities were limited. When a student's propensity for lying and stealing came up in the assessment, it resulted in denial and defensiveness while the child in question sat in the meeting wearing a knowing grin. One kid's dark talent launched him to become a cult leader who instigated sexual deviance and murder among his followers.

The school assigned teachers based on the factors I revealed and became their mentors until they graduated from high school. The qualification to be one of these advisors was simply that I saw in them the ability to guide and help students consider what to do with their gifts. Members of the school board valued my insights as they pertained to both students and faculty, giving me the power to accept or deny someone an opportunity.

A balance of both light and dark appeared in many children. These were the ones for whom it was hardest to predict an outcome with accuracy. But wouldn't that mean that they had unseen potential to do what was right for them? Was it possible to express both dark and light abilities in their chosen life path?

I identified their natural inclinations, the gifts they were born with, their ultimate fate, and then turned it over to the advisors to help them reach their potential, their true destiny. But destiny is a choice. They could succumb to their fate based on what I saw and shared, even though it was still possible to change it. Sometimes I wondered if using my talent to see potential was ethical. Was it fair to pigeonhole a person into a pre-determined destiny based on intuition? Should instructions include how to decide between courses of action to use their innate abilities in new ways, such as shifting the dark talents of the cult leader to become a positive influence on society?

Questions continued to plague me. I had guided the destinies of hundreds of children and staff over the years. Did I have the right to do so? Was my gift for seeing potential an adequate trait to wield this much power over others? My visions of who had the intelligence and compassion to become a doctor affected all those that doctor treated. How much of what I saw was inaccurate? The judgment I placed upon students and teachers impacted the parents and those they interacted with; a ripple effect that could help or harm. Were there better candidates for medical school than those I chose?

People trusted my insights as absolute and looked no further into what their lives might hold for them. I had to see for myself whether a different outcome was possible, so one day, I approached my responsibilities differently.

I started by evaluating a boy named Johnny. He was excited to meet with me. We sat in my office facing each other in plexiglass chairs designed to expose the entire student. The messages I'd get about an individual could come across from anywhere in the body or from their energy field. The potential for Johnny's life swirled about him. I waited until certain aspects of his most likely tendencies settled and saw him lying on a bench with a book open on top of him. The scene struck me as laziness, not being serious about his studies. He was one of those students who had a mix of energies that could go in many directions. How much of what I imparted had to do with my own impressions and beliefs?

Using my revised approach, I realized just how much interpretation was necessary in determining the fates of the people I evaluated. It disturbed me to think I may have misinterpreted what I saw and how it affected so many lives.

I shifted my perspective and saw Johnny as a hardworking student, exhausted from studying and taking a much-needed break. He was dreaming about a life at sea, studying wildlife and addressing issues that threatened the environment. Johnny's energy of both light and dark became clear to me as addressing the problems of pollution and the threat it presented to the animals and birds that relied on the ocean. He was the light addressing the dark. My body validated this new interpretation with a solid sensation that differed from previous experience. Understanding flooded my senses. Had I used my gifts incorrectly all these years?

Now I saw the backlash of my misplaced confidence rippling through the world; my misguided advice and the seriousness of using my insights alone to determine the futures of so many.

I shared my vision with Johnny, who lit up with joy. He loved reading about life at sea and how the environment was being compromised by dumping trash and other toxic waste into the ocean. He dreamed of developing natural and mechanical solutions that cleaned the waste and renewed wildlife populations. As he spoke, I saw it transpire before my eyes. He would accomplish these goals beyond his expectations. Johnny hugged me and ran to tell his parents. I submitted my report to them and assigned him teachers with expertise in engineering and environmental issues.

There was a renewed sense of my purpose within this meeting. It was truly about the purpose of each person and how they were best to serve humanity.

Because of this experience, I wrote an inclusive process for evaluation where my impressions were part of a broader assessment that included the hopes and dreams of the student and their favorite subjects to study. The recommendation also suggested including teacher observations of the student and how we could assist the individual in areas of struggle.

With these in place, the school brightened as I had never seen before. Students were happy in their studies and faculty enjoyed their role in the development of their charges. Their potential destinies were no longer guided by the ideas of one man, but shared among all those involved to create the brightest futures possible for each person and for the world.

Samuel's Expanded Awareness

Samuel sighed, struck by the wisdom of the teacher and how he sought to inspire others in the end. To recognize his own error and limitations was a profoundly wise thing to admit. He wondered what Andy Bartholemew would see in him. He had a hard time seeing himself objectively and would welcome intuitive insights into his nature. Working for others his whole life hadn't led him to what his purpose was. Maybe that's what his mother hoped he'd find here, in this cemetery or in the new town he'd moved to.

Samuel rolled the scroll, tying it with the ribbon, then held it under the low branches and allowed the tree to absorb its story. The sun sat lower in the sky. Time to leave before the darkness set in.

He had enough for one day anyhow. Samuel left the remains of the sunshine behind and stepped carefully through the undergrowth into the darkening woods. His head swiveled, checking for signs of the hooded figure that drove him to the hazel tree. A sense of relief washed over him when he reached the iron gates of Willow Ponds Cemetery. His body fully relaxed as he sat in his old Volvo with the seatbelt fastened tightly around him, having a grounding effect. Once again, his was the only vehicle in the visitors' parking lot.

He pulled onto the road and headed to the house that wasn't quite like home just yet. It took less than five minutes to drive through the downtown area where the grocery store, bookstore, clothing shop, and pharmacy stood. He shopped for food on Fridays and it was only Tuesday, so he zipped by, eager to resume unpacking his belongings. The purge of his childhood home was a boon for Purple Heart, where he donated the bulk of Charlotte's and his belongings. It was hard leaving civilization and its conveniences behind. The new house was much smaller than his childhood home, so it was necessary to pare down his stuff.

Samuel watched squirrels and a few deer run along the side of the road. In this rural area, many small houses had lots of acres around them, a bonus for living in the middle of nowhere. His own vintage country cottage sat on almost twelve acres, giving him privacy he never had living in a bustling town. He pulled into his long, gravel driveway. Large windows were nestled in white siding. A stone chimney poked out from the center of the house. The wood-burning fireplace heated the entire building. This year, he had logs delivered to last him all winter, but next year, he planned to chop it himself. With all the trees on the property, he expected to lose a few in storms, so he'd use them as firewood.

He'd never cut down a healthy tree, especially now that the cemetery taught him that a tree is not always just a tree. The idea of dryads came to him. His mother told him stories about them; spirits living in trees, their life force connected to a specific tree, usually in a sacred grove. It was as if Willow Ponds Cemetery consisted entirely of sacred groves, each spot in its five hundred acres having its own energy, its own sense of timelessness.

He parked the car in front of the main house and glanced over at the tiny caretaker's cottage. A smaller version of the main house, Samuel still contemplated whether to use it for his own as-yet-to-be-determined purposes or whether to actually hire a caretaker. He'd only been living here a couple of months and wanted to wait to see how he dealt with living alone with no real neighbors to speak of. There was time to decide. Nothing but time.

He entered the house, popped a frozen dinner of eggplant parmesan into the microwave, and unpacked one of the smaller boxes holding his mother's favorite knick-knacks for the living room shelves. The microwave beeped, signaling the end of unpacking for the night. He preferred to chip away at the task rather than hurriedly distributing his belongings throughout the house. Samuel ate in front of the television and relaxed enough to sleep well that evening.

But the next morning, the anticipation of what he'd encounter in the Forest of the Dead brought the tension back, although not enough to prevent his curiosity from being satisfied. Samuel let his nose lead the way today. The fresh smell of pine beckoned him. A pine grove was in a section of the cemetery that he had not explored. Planted parallel to one another, five on each side, they formed a walkway softened with pine needles. One of them called his name and delivered a small leather-bound book decorated with strange symbols in black ink from its rough bark. The bed of pine needles invited him to sit, excited for the next story to unfold.

The Tattoo Artist
Pine: Purification & Creative Expression

I'm Natalie Hathaway, a fifth-generation tattoo artist known in esoteric inkers circles around the globe. My reputation among those who design and ink special, secret, and unique tattoos on clientele is unequaled. I've created protection symbols that shield its owner from emotional, psychological, physical, and spiritual attacks. Skin memorials of the deceased use ink mixed with their ashes, enabling them to speak to and guide them when asked. My art is ancient and meaningful, especially because I use techniques unique to my family. The approach is a secret process that only a few besides my family have learned through apprenticeship. In thirty years of doing this work, I've only trained one carefully selected artist.

Part of me struggles with the ethics of capturing the dead inside the image. I never know whose ashes I'm mixing with the ink. Even though I interview the client before starting the work, they may not be honest with me. The art that comes when I use the ink is unique to that blend. It's not an image that the customer chooses; it comes out of me as I align with the energy of the ashes. To delve into the person's nature isn't always a pleasant experience. It can jar me, affecting my balance for days afterward. The loveliest energy comes from clients who bring me the ashes of their beloved pets. This is the purist of sensations; not at all like humans.

It can take hours to produce the image on the skin depending on the design and color selection. If it is a simple line drawing of a protection symbol in black ink, it comes out in an hour or less, as long as I'm channeling the image. Many gang members refer their colleagues to me, trusting that my designs hold the power to protect them.

I've learned to read the types of threats a client may face and design their tattoo accordingly. I share my evaluation with the customer to make sure I get it right. Some clients have energy that frightens me, especially in my work with the occult. I get practitioners looking to enhance their power in ways that would cause harm. When I sense this type of client, I turn them away. They might threaten me, but the karmic backlash would be worse than anything they could throw at me. On the flip side of the coin, I get benevolent clients who come with an open heart. My work with them goes smoothly and turns out beautifully.

Integrity is paramount in my business. As an artist, I abide by strict rules handed down within my family on how to do the work. That isn't the case for some customers who walk through my door.

Rumors swirled in the artist community about a customer who gets a tattoo and then the artist dies within three days of doing the work. This has happened six times so far. We don't know if the intention to do harm was present in this client. The only way to identify the energy was to see them in person. The potential to tattoo the person known as *the cursed client* had the inkers' community on edge. For the sake of the inkers' community, I decided some recon was in order to find out what images this customer received. It was the only way to help identify this person.

I researched the names of the dead artists and then called those tattoo parlors and asked about the last client that particular artist worked on before they passed, what image they drew, and where they placed it. The deceased tattooers lived and worked within a twenty-mile radius of one another. My parlor was within that geographic area, so the odds of meeting *the cursed client* were high.

The first parlor I contacted said that their artist, Stoney, took on a male client a couple of hours before closing time. He was tall and muscular. No one heard him say his name, but they remembered he chose a skull with a snake winding through it, all in black ink. The last time they saw Stoney, he was working on the guy's forearm. He lived long enough to snap a photo of his work. All but one staff member remained when the guy left and, despite her calling 911, Stoney was dead on arrival. The hospital said it was a widow-maker heart attack. Stoney was only thirty-eight years old. The image was common; the skull represented death, and the snake symbolized the metaphorical death of the old self before the new way of being comes forward.

I next called upon the business where another artist's life ended. His co-workers described the same guy as the first place I called. No one remembered the client's name. This time, he asked for a raven on his other forearm, using black ink only. The staff described it as the most realistic raven the artist ever produced, each feather clear, with the wings down. It looked like it would fly right off his arm. Again, he took a photo, as is the custom to put in the artist's showcase for future customers to view. The raven symbolized the shapeshifter, the magician within, able to manifest one's desires. Then the artist retreated to the back room where employees found him dead fifteen minutes later. Again, an unlikely heart attack in a man in his late twenties.

I contacted each shop on the list, and the staff described the same person in each case, always asking for designs representing death and transformation. In one case, he requested the image of the Death card in tarot on his upper arm above the raven. In another, he wanted the cycles of the moon across his chest. On his other arm above the skull, he chose a vulture, the symbol of death and rebirth, but also of purification. Every circumstance was the same; the artists, all males, dropped dead of a heart attack. No intervention could have helped them recover.

I pulled up all the images on my computer screen side-by-side. The photos showed only body parts with images, no face to go along with them. While the theme of death came through, it seemed the intention was to transform it into something else. Maybe it took the energy of death for *the cursed client* to manifest the transformation he wanted. It didn't seem like malice was inherent in the situation. Instead, he wanted ultimate change within himself.

I sent the images to tattoo parlors within twenty miles as a caution with a request to send this customer my way. Replies of thanks ensued for the fear fellow artists had affected their creativity. Armed with information about this client, I slipped into a meditative state, asking the universe to send me the image to transform him in the way he wanted; in a way that he could accomplish his goals without threat to the artist. The perfect image floated in, and I drew furiously to make sure I captured it as Spirit intended. It was both a transformative symbol and a protection.

A few days later, the person known as *the cursed client* walked through my door. He matched the description perfectly. His body art was where the other tattooists placed it. His boyish face on a giant man's body showed a dichotomy that he likely tried to overcome. I told him to lie on his stomach so I could give him the symbol he needed to fully transform. I warned him that the colors I planned to use would hurt a bit more than black ink alone. He was fine with it.

I worked on him for seven hours, perfecting each detail. As I marked his skin, visions of his curses, life's disappointments, mistakes, losses, and regrets flashed in my mind as though the memories were my own. Each time I added a piece of the image, those flashes lessened, with some obliterated in time with the movement of the needles. The man's negative memories lightened. He breathed easier and even fell asleep for a bit.

At the end of the session, I sat back and admired my work. One of my staff photographed it, astonished by the realism achieved with ink. The majestic maple tree image sent branches reaching across his upper back and roots cascading down his spine. Maples balance the energy between masculine and feminine within the person to achieve greater intuition, creativity, and health. The red leaves, black and brown trunk and branches, and yellow sunlight beaming from behind it held the energy of growth, hope, transformation, and enlightenment. These are the vibrations he needed to achieve balance and live a productive and joyful life. I completed the design with a proprietary protection symbol hidden in the roots and sigils representing powerful benevolent entities to watch over him, concealed within the twisty bark of the ancient maple.

He looked at his back using two mirrors and broke into a wide, bright smile, paid in cash, and thanked me. I never got his name, but I lived for decades afterward.

Samuel's Rite of Passage

Samuel was glad that Natalie survived the ordeal of the cursed client. It struck him how brave she was—and confident—to get him what he needed while no longer putting others at risk. As he held the closed book between the palms of his hands, he realized he had bonded with the spirits of these trees, as though they were real friends.

He looked down at his bare arms and wondered if he should get a tattoo. He was pretty sure it would be the image of a tree.

There was still time for one more story before heading home, so he walked over to visit his mother and noticed her tree had grown another couple of feet. It was now as tall as he was at six feet. Would Charlotte's tree eventually produce a book or a scroll for him to read?

In the meantime, there were plenty of other stories for the trees to share with him. A copse of silver birch trees stood nearby, their ghostly white trunks and dark accents apparent among the darker trunks surrounding them. Samuel's heart raced in anticipation of the story waiting for him. He retrieved the book waiting for him in the grass at the base of the tallest silver birch and made himself comfortable.

The Coach

Silver Birch: Awakening of New Life

I, Hailey Campbell, started my coaching practice out of graduate school. My clients were open to feedback and guidance, trusting me to listen intently and identify patterns that held them back from living their best life. I enjoyed my work and loved seeing my clients get rid of self-sabotaging thoughts and behaviors and replace them with positive action.

Each week, we'd meet by phone for an hour, review the practice assignments from the previous week, and make gradual progress in each session. One client, who we'll call Emily, called each week at precisely seven o'clock in the evening. For two years, we filled each session with laughter, tears, insights, and transformation.

I could sense when she'd pull back and when she opened, when we were treading in sensitive territory and when we could joke about her approach to a situation. Her voice was so familiar to me I could hear it hitch if she was upset or sweeten when she was happy. The rhythm of our sessions came easily, even when the topic was rough. And we made progress. Lots of it.

One evening, the phone rang exactly at seven o'clock, as Emily always did. She sounded upset and depressed, her voice a whisper, like it was difficult to speak. After determining that she was not ill, she explained how lonely she'd been. I asked when this started. She had never complained of loneliness before. In fact, her relationships had gotten better since she entered coaching. I probed for more information, trying to determine if someone had hurt her. She insisted that wasn't the case. The session ended with even more questions than I had in the beginning.

The following week, Emily was right on time for our call. She said her loneliness persisted and that she could not communicate with people. Was it with a particular group of people? Was she using the techniques we practiced in the past to connect with people and have a positive interaction? She let out a wail that chilled me to the bone. It sounded like she was in an echo chamber, the way a blip in technology can do. I asked her if she was on a speakerphone or using ear buds and a microphone. She said no. I asked her to interact only with those she was most comfortable with for the next week and see how that felt.

The third week, at precisely seven in the evening, the phone rang. It was Emily, sobbing. I asked what was wrong. She said she didn't know. It was like she was in a void and had no one to talk to except me. That wasn't healthy. We needed to find a solution, but I didn't know what the problem was. I pulled up her social media page to see if there were any clues.

And there it was. Emily's obituary and her profile page turned into a memorial. In bold, next to her name at the top of the page, was the word *Remembering*.

My jaw dropped. I could still hear her crying. I spoke in a soothing voice and asked how she had died. An apartment fire started in the unit next to hers and spread through the building. Emily was asleep and had no fire alarm. She complained that there was nothing around her, no people, no furniture, nothing. I assured her we would get through this as we had gotten through so many other challenges in her life.

Remembering a book I read years ago about helping spirits cross over, I located it in my bookcase. The ritual required a white candle, which I had in a drawer. After blessing it with a prayer from the book, I lit the candle and asked Emily if she could see the light. She said yes. Guiding her, I could sense her moving, gliding toward the light. The assurance that loved ones who crossed before were waiting to welcome her encouraged her toward the unknown. I hoped that was true.

She became excited, saying she could see her grandmother and her favorite pet. I smiled, feeling her joy. Her voice faded as her last words of thanks came through the phone. She was gone. My journey with her through life allowed me to help her in death. I would miss her.

Samuel's New Perspective

Samuel felt sad for Emily, in her oblivion, and grateful that Natalie was there for her at the end, not put off by death or speaking to the dead, but with a strong desire to help, regardless of the form her client took.

The dead took various forms as his surroundings made clear to him. He wondered if the figure he saw yesterday was a ghost or something that had never been human. Did the sighting mean that he could see the dead? No matter, it gave him chills to think of it and hoped he'd never see it again. One and done.

Movement in the woods up ahead pulled Samuel from his thoughts. The object flashed and turned into a red-tailed hawk that flew right at him. Before he could rise from his seated position and run, the hawk was upon him. Samuel's fear was unfounded. The hawk perched on his shoulder; sharp nails dug in for balance.

He relaxed and allowed the experience to guide him. The raptor was exquisite, powerful, and surprisingly light. It was a pleasant sensation. Maybe the claws piercing through his T-shirt and into his skin were similar to Natalie's tattoo needles. He wished she was still alive to put a tattoo on him. A magical tree tattoo.

The hawk hunkered down and sprung briskly off his shoulder into the darkest part of the woods.

Watching it fly with precision, Samuel's eye caught a row of poplar trees creating a border between the eastern and western section of the cemetery. One stood out to Samuel, and he approached it with curiosity about the story waiting to be told. He pulled the life record from the dense branches, its hard cover imprinted with the image of a house. A nearby patch of moss called to him, so he sat and readied himself for the next adventure.

The Realtor
Poplar: Strong Foundation & Great Rewards

I, Harry Goodwin, was a realtor of the highest order. I sold houses large and small, vacant lots, townhouses, and condominiums. They all had one thing in common: they all matched the energies of the buyer. You see, I had a knack for seeing alignments between a dwelling and the person destined to live there.

If I had a dollar for every time a homeowner said, "This place is perfect!" I'd be wealthier than I've gotten from selling properties. They didn't know that I could sense energy that prevented a house from being sold or that drained their vitality.

Energy in a home builds up from arguments among the residents, anger, depression, and anxiety. The property, with or without a building on it, absorbs these dense emotions and buyers would feel it. They'd feel repelled or drained but weren't sure why, especially when they liked the overall space and location.

Meeting with a client gave me the chance to see their energy and to feel what type of house would align with it. If they had a specific style of home in mind, it might take longer to find or build from scratch. Sometimes, I'd have to manipulate the energy among available homes to fit their needs. Most times, I found the place the buyers resonated with by their specified move date.

After closing, we'd celebrate at a place that knew me well. The proprietors asked if this was the latest client to celebrate their perfect new home, saying it loud enough that customers sitting at surrounding tables would hear and ask for my card. There was no need to advertise with my latest satisfied clients there to sing my praises. My grandfather always said that it's better to have others sing your praises than to brag about yourself.

After one of these celebrations, a new customer came up to me and asked for a meeting right there in the restaurant. The man had a musty odor about him, as though his tweed jacket had been in storage for an exceedingly long time. He was having difficulty finding the perfect property. The ideal place would be rustic, maybe with a thatched roof or the modern version of such, and nestled in the woods. A country cottage. Privacy was the goal. The location was flexible, as was the cost, as long as it was within the state of Pennsylvania. I envisioned the type of house he sought and used my mind's eye to see the house appropriate for his distinctive energy, different from any I had previously encountered.

It was unusual to hear such broad criteria, but his insistence about the type of property gave me the utmost opportunity to find him the right place. So, I searched agent-listed and for-sale-by-owner properties. I drove around rural areas to see which properties fit the bill, whether or not they were for sale, prepared to knock on the door and ask if the owner had an inclination to sell.

Only one property stood out as the perfect place for this client. Oddly, he had described my house as though he had been there and fallen in love with it as I had. I had an intimate knowledge and sense of the energy there and could actually see the house and his energy fitting together nicely. But my place was dear to me and imprinted with my energy signature. The large trees, a half-acre pond, the stone cottage that contained a library room complete with a cozy fireplace, sitting perfectly centered on the wooded twenty acres. Peace. Quiet. Mine.

I probably could ask a great deal of money for it. I had no one to consult. No wife or children. Only myself to contend with.

What if I brought him to my house to see his reaction? More than that, what would be the house's reaction to him? I hadn't considered that the house had a choice. Maybe that's what happened more times than I realized, that the house itself decided it didn't like the energy of the buyer.

Whenever I was home, it was a sacred space, a sanctuary from the stresses of the day. My vitality increased when I was there, and I slept well even after the most difficult workday. The house loved me, didn't it?

Questions swirled in my mind. Should I take a chance that it might like someone else better? What if it chose the client over me? Was it possible that the client could change the energy of my property to fit his own needs the way I'd done so many times for others? Would it be foolish to take a chance?

I walked through the rooms of my beloved house and sensed how it responded to me. It reacted as it always had, as far as I could tell. No amount of money was worth giving up my haven.

Not wanting to disappoint the client, I continued searching for properties, as well as looking into the client himself. The address he gave me at our initial meeting came up as a cemetery close to the restaurant where I met him. A longshot at best, I searched for the headstone of my client, Charles Walker. In the vast graveyard, the hope of finding him quickly was unlikely. I spotted a caretaker and engaged his assistance. We found Mr. Walker closest to the church building. The man had expired in 1902. The stone read: *His body lies here, but his soul rests in the woods.* Strange to be sure.

And then I realized it would be prudent to research where he had lived before his death. Imagine my shock to find that Charles Walker was the original owner of my property and built the home I now lived in.

Samuel's Dawning Outlook

S amuel smiled, thinking of his new home and wondering if this story had any connection to it. It sounded similar, for sure. He could always do the research with the town hall records to discover its history. If Charles Walker and Harry Goodwin were on the property records, it would blow him away. He wasn't sure he wanted to know.

He thought of his mother, Charlotte, and how the stories of the trees would fascinate her. She'd likely see them in a way that included elements of justice, as she was the most sought-after attorney in their area. It may have been the reason he never knew his father. Charlotte was not only an unassailable person but also a powerful lawyer, winning case after case. Her practice focused on women who others took advantage of. She intimidated men.

Samuel often thought that she likely used his father simply to get pregnant and sometimes wondered about him. She certainly didn't need his money, if he had any. He was never in their lives, and she never spoke of him. The vocation of his unknown parent stoked his imagination. It might give him an indication of what his own gifts were. His curiosity about his father extended to the origin of his own skin, being one or two shades deeper than his Caucasian mother. One day, he might take a DNA test, but for now, he'd let his mysterious origin persist. Charlotte always told her son how beautiful he was and that his dark hair and eyes and exotic look made her want to kiss his face, which she did when they were alone. She spared him from embarrassment in front of his friends.

Charlotte's influence filled every aspect of his life. She was his teacher, his advisor, and the one who showered him with love. She made sure he was happy and fulfilled, encouraging him to find his own path rather than imposing one on him. His mother told him to talk to the trees to find his way. Now she had put him in a position to do just that.

A giant ash tree signaled him to walk across a clearing and learn its story. Its branches spread twenty feet across and one hundred feet tall, relishing the sunlight. The stems had six pairs of tapered leaves with branches growing from a trunk whose bark made diamond patterns due to its age. Samuel knew that the tree had lived a long time, its strength and stability permeating the clearing. He looked forward to seeing what type of strength the spirit in this tree possessed. He looked up into the oval-shaped canopy and saw a document balanced on a branch. Reaching up, he saw the pages glue-bound on the left side; the cover had a simple design with a curlicue above the name. The form taken by each book gave Samuel clues as to the type of person the spirit had been. With his back to the tree trunk and backside nestled between the roots, Samuel journeyed along with the author.

The Doctor
Ash: Healing & Self-mastery

Designated as an important part of my community, I, Hal Ashwood, have treated the people where I live for everything from the common cold to delivering babies for decades. They call me *Doc* and trust me with their health and their secrets.

My mother taught me about natural medicine, saying that healthcare practiced in hospitals needed supplemental intervention. I studied science and the ways of Western medicine to understand how the two came together. The medicinal mushrooms and other sacred plants on the hill behind our house spoke to me, telling me how to use them and when to harvest them. I'd sit for hours on the mossy ground just listening and writing what they said. They taught me the importance of the cardinal directions and how those points related to specific illnesses. Most of the lessons were about balance and harmony between natural remedies and their uses within the context of a hospital setting.

The herb garden behind my practice allowed me to develop medicines we'd have to drive hours to obtain from a hospital or pharmacy. Sometimes it was hard to manage without help, but most of the time I got by since house calls made up the bulk of my practice.

When entering a patient's home, I noted its condition, the smells present, the attitudes and energies of others in the home, and how they responded to the ill person. These factors contributed to the state of the patient, gave an indication as to how the illness came about, and the likely speed of their recovery. If they got loving care, they recuperated much faster than if the caregiver resented having to stay home and play nurse. If mold was present, spores could be the origin of the malady. A clean home fostered healing while a dirty house dragged out the sickness.

Sunshine was part of my prescription, moving the patient to a comfortable chair outdoors for fresh air and for the body to produce Vitamin D to aid in the immune response. Flower essences aligned with the person's vibration helped calm their anxiety, overcame insomnia, and worked with other medication to address symptoms such as coughing and sneezing.

I sat with my patients, patting their hand and speaking in a soothing voice. The more they trusted me, the more cooperative they were in following my instructions.

One day, a virus spread throughout the residents, young and old. Schools were closed. Businesses shut their doors. But I stayed open. I made a batch of my protection remedy and drank it down so I could go door to door treating symptoms and collecting information about the illness without getting sick myself.

Whatever caused the sickness made them weak, nauseous, feverish, and gave them body aches in every joint. The locals called it "The Plague." I tried various remedies to see which one worked, jotting down the age and gender of the person, along with their symptoms, and administering the one that seemed to work. Most folks were back to near full health within two weeks.

And then I got a call from a frantic neighbor of a seventy-something year old resident named Jed who needed care. After my successes with my other patients, I was confident that the plant spirits would guide me to help him.

When I arrived, the house was quiet. He was the last of his line and had no one to care for him. With no insurance to speak of, he couldn't hire a nurse. My services were free to those in his situation. He was weaker than others with the virus, and he had an additional unwholesome frequency pulsing through him. Death whispered to me, letting me know Jed's condition was dire. He was giving up. The patient's desire to live was an essential component in the ability to recover. My will alone couldn't bring him back from the brink of demise.

Jed's full beard was scraggly, he was underweight, and his eyes were bleary. The sour smell of sickness, trash, soiled bed linens, and dirty dishes exacerbated his condition. I felt it. I smelled it. My heart sank as I entered his bedroom, where he lay still. Squeezing his hand, I got permission to help him to a chair so I could strip the bed, put on clean sheets and a fresh blanket I found in the closet, and give him a thorough sponge bath. I washed his hair and beard over a bucket, brushed his teeth, and got him back into bed. He had a faint smile and his energy lifted slightly.

I took out the trash, swept the floor, did the dishes, and opened the windows. My actions and the movement of fresh air cleared the foul smell. A can of chicken noodle soup was in the cabinet, so I heated it in a mug and fed him while he sat in bed.

We quietly talked of the weather, how long he'd been ill, the sadness that overcame him after his wife of fifty years died two months ago, and how he had no one to care for him. He told me how he was ready to die before I came over. I asked if he realized that a lovely neighbor named Lillian called me to check on him and that she was worried, but didn't want to disturb him if he was grieving. She knew of his heart condition and wanted to make sure he was taking his medicine.

Jed's eyes brightened. I smiled and gave him the remedies he required. He promised to rest. I promised to let Lillian know she could visit.

A week later, I was in town and saw Jed, walking arm-in-arm with Lillian. They were picking out fruit and vegetables at the grocery store. Jed had trimmed his hair and beard. He wore a bright smile and said something that made Lillian laugh. To be polite, I asked how he was doing, although I already knew. His vitality was apparent from the smell of soap and his healthy complexion. And while he shook my hand and thanked me for healing him, the truth was he needed love and compassion, and his body did the rest.

Samuel's Healing Path

Samuel thought about Charlotte and whether he had given her enough love and attention. Maybe she would have lived longer if he had. But her secretive nature hid her health issues from him. Could it be that it was a test of how much he cared? He couldn't imagine she'd question his devotion to her. Besides, she was the queen of self-care, getting regular massages and having help to keep the house exactly how she liked it.

The story reminded him of how his mother took him to the woods to teach him about the plants and the trees. That was his primary memory of their time together whenever she wasn't working, which she did most of the time. Her cases were complex, and she didn't wish that type of vocational life for him. She wanted him tied to nature, to his intuitive senses, and to search for his gifts. That was difficult to do living in the city. He didn't want to open himself to the energies of so many people and their stressful lives. The only time it seemed safe to open his senses was in the woods; that's why Charlotte took him there as often as she could. And now he lived in the country at her behest, a much more peaceful existence than he would have had otherwise.

Samuel saw the value of being separate from lots of people. He'd found his intuitive sense much stronger. Or maybe it was being in this forested cemetery. Was he picking up the energies of the tree spirits? He certainly was alone here, except for the hooded figure he'd seen before, but not since. Samuel kept an eye out for any other sightings of what he thought of as *spirit walkers,* especially when chills rolled down his back, prompting him to check behind him.

His mind shifted to his mother's sycamore tree, and he strolled over to check on its progress. It had sprung up another four feet in height and its trunk was growing thicker. He smiled at the thought of holding his mother's book of life in his hands and also had a rush of fear at what he might discover. He pushed the thought aside for now and moved in a direction as yet unexplored.

Up ahead, white flowers peeked through the branches. Samuel recognized it as a dogwood. This one, heavy with blossoms, usually bloomed in spring, yet now, in the humidity of August, the tree thrived. His mother told him that the flowers were actually modified leaves, but he preferred to think of them as blossoms.

He retrieved the scroll from the center of the dense tree and sat on the bench that appeared a moment before.

The Hermit

Flowering Dogwood: Secrets, Protection, & Illusion

My name is Harold Kramer, but I'm known as *The Hermit*. Having chosen to live apart from others, without connection to technology, I've become a curiosity, with some still making the trek through the woods to get a peek at the man who lives alone in a tiny cottage surrounded by a dense flower garden, a vegetable patch, and a picket fence. Some brave souls attempt to make conversation. After assessing them, I decide whether to waste my breath engaging with them. Usually, I nod a silent greeting and go inside.

The decision to change my lifestyle came after a particularly tough week at work. The noise of the city and the increasing number of rude, abusive individuals at the office, on the roads, and at the grocery store. They came at me in the media, in politics, and in corporate leadership. It was no longer possible to live with these types of energies. I grew progressively more tired and less tolerant of humanity and the toxic individuals and intentions surrounding me. Even my Labrador retriever, Bogart, seemed anxious.

Some people are good despite the rising trend in self-absorption, intolerance of those who are different, and their sense of entitlement, but there are not enough of them to shift the balance. How could I depend on society at the rate it was going?

It was time to block out external forces and become self-sufficient. The need to experience quiet and listen to my soul before deciding if a life apart was for me or whether I needed to go back to the land of unmanageable society was apparent. A simple life, quiet reflection, and meditation were in order to hear my inner voice. And for me to become more self-aware in the process. I hadn't taken the time to discover truly who I was.

Would I be lonely in my self-imposed isolation or gain strength I'd never attained before? To experience resilience developed through facing the challenges of living outside of daily conveniences and the ability to survive without it had the potential to boost my endurance. I had no significant other to consider in this decision, only Bogart, and he was happy as long as we were together.

I found a furnished remote cottage with indoor plumbing, water from a well, and electricity from a solar power system. My belongings were mainly books, bedding, and a few decorative items, along with Bogart's toys and bed.

For these last five years, I've enjoyed the company of woodland animals, Bogart, and the thrill of seeing the myriad stars in the heavens. Without bombardment of bad news from morning until night, I'm less stressed and distressed, my heart is lighter, and what I now consider necessities are at arm's length from my cottage door.

Yet, there were times when I yearned for a companion, one woman, to share our deepest thoughts and hopes. The idea of one special person with whom to have an intimate connection and share my sanctuary lived side-by-side with the fear of destroying the peace I'd cultivated. Being alone was better than being with the wrong one. That inner conflict tore at me, along with knowing that I'd have to venture into a populated area to find someone who wanted to be with me and live the way I did. Admittedly, I wasn't the easiest person to live with. Then it occurred to me I could use harmonious vibrations to attract the right person to my cottage.

I shaved for the first time in months, bathed Bogart, and organized the cottage, putting items in pairs to draw the vibration of partnership. I focused on the desire to be with someone rather than the fear. My bookshelves contained stories of people connecting at a deep level, and I read those while waiting for my right relationship to manifest.

Weeks passed. One day, I heard twigs snapping. Bogart stood on alert but didn't bark. I watched the path in front of the cottage for movement. And there she was. A woman in her mid-forties, same as me, dressed in jeans, a flannel shirt, and a long, brown ponytail sticking out from under her knit hat. Her collie came bounding toward Bogart, and they sniffed each other, tails wagging.

She smiled and waved. I did the same. It was magnetic. Bogart greeted the stranger and led her to where I stood. She introduced herself as Margaret as she gave me a firm handshake.

Margaret accepted my offering of homegrown yarrow tea with honey from my hives, and we chatted amiably as old friends would. Her knowledge of teas and their properties fascinated me; sharing that the yarrow we were drinking was good for inflammation and digestion, but not if you're allergic to ragweed. We watched the dogs playing. I hadn't realized that Bogart was eager for a friend, too.

As the sun descended toward the horizon, I offered her a bed for the night. She chose to beat the sun back home, promising to return soon. Even without Margaret there, her presence remained.

In the early afternoon the following day, Margaret and her collie, Roxy, walked up the path to my cottage. They were a welcome sight to behold. From her backpack, she pulled out a bag filled with sandwiches, chips, and cans of ginger ale. I was ravenous at the smell of food from town, which I hadn't had in years. I knew I'd pay for it later with an upset stomach and hoped the yarrow tea would soothe it.

But for now, I ate heartily as we talked; I explained what made me live away from people. She commiserated to a point, saying living with the conveniences of town was important to her with breaks hiking in the woods. That's how she found my cottage. She hadn't heard the local legend of *The Hermit* and happened upon me by accident. I knew it was destiny, not chance, that brought her to me.

Weeks turned to months, with Margaret and Roxy visiting on weekends, many times bringing food she liked, and occasionally spending the night. I re-acclimated to prepared food, but still preferred fresh vegetables from my garden; most times I included my salad or vegetable stew as part of the meal.

She told me about her executive job in an office, just as I had in my former life, and we compared notes. The discussion made my throat tense and stomach tighten. There was so much more to life than making money. I had enough to live on into my nineties and owned my property, so didn't need to be part of that world. Each time she saw me, she encouraged me to come home with her to see if the world was any different from when I left. From what she shared with me of the news, I highly doubted that, but she convinced me that our relationship couldn't move forward without compromise, and I reluctantly agreed.

So, we picked a day to meet in Margaret's world. I set to venture out of the woods with Bogart. It provoked severe anxiety. No one was around, but my world was the cottage and the privacy of the woods. As I walked down the winding trail, away from my sanctuary, my heart beat faster and my breath became shallow. I bent down and reached for Bogart, petting him to steady myself. We trekked farther down the trail on shaking legs.

A few miles into the hike, the scent of the woods changed to the odors of humans, various foods, and industry. These smells tainted the clean air I was accustomed to. Thoughts of what created them rose in my mind. Teeth clenched, I took a few more steps before turning around and heading for my haven.

The realization that I found my purpose, my life, and my nature consumed me as I drew closer to the cottage. It was heaven on earth. How could I desire more than what I had? Gratitude lit my heart with contentment. The respite with Margaret had grown tiresome once she insisted I go back to what I'd left behind if I expected our relationship to continue. The idea of doing what she required of me reflected the reason I became *The Hermit*. I had finally found myself and lived independently, content with my existence. Peace was paramount to living.

Margaret never returned, probably realizing, as I had, that our separate worlds were exactly what we wanted and where we were supposed to be. No one should compromise a life perfectly aligned to their nature. From then on, Bogart and I welcomed the occasional visitor, inviting them for tea, and sharing my insights on life. Unwittingly guided here, they came to get a message meant just for them to help navigate their life. Then I'd send them on their merry way, knowing they were better off for having met *The Hermit*.

Samuel's Shifting

The search for satisfaction was one that Samuel was familiar with. He hadn't had any strong attachments except to his mother and never knew his father, but didn't long for any either. It made him wonder if he was heading for a life as a hermit. Charlotte taught him to go with the flow, so he would do that for now. All that he learned from the tree spirits would likely shift his path. For now, he settled into his new circumstances faster than expected.

He walked back toward the denser part of the forest, wishing his mother's tree grew thicker, impatient for the availability of her life book. Upon strolling past her sycamore, it looked larger than before, but not big enough to produce her story. Hunger prompted him to head home to eat and come back that evening. He hadn't seen these woods in the dark and was curious.

When he pulled into the empty parking area, a soft glow greeted him. With a backpack filled with water and snacks, Samuel was ready to spend the night in the forest. A waxing gibbous moon shone brightly as it climbed higher in the sky and cast shadows on the ground.

The forest sighed, welcoming him like an old friend. It seemed glad he returned during the evening. In his mind, this was not a cemetery, but a living entity. Samuel realized it had something new to show him.

Small circles of multi-colored light bubbled from the trees; likely spirit orbs. Some trees glowed along their branches. The brightest shimmer came from the darkest part of the forest. The closed wrought-iron gate radiated the colors that moved beyond it. There was no need for the flashlight he brought with him. He pushed the stiff gate open and slipped through.

The first place he wanted to see was Charlotte's tree. Chills filled his body when he saw the bright green light beaming from its branches and trunk, thickening and strengthening them. No wonder it grew so fast. He reached out and held his hand over the emanation and noticed a powerful vibration go into his hand and up his arm. Unsure of how it would affect him, he yanked his hand back and rubbed it. After inspecting his arm, no change occurred from the interaction. He thanked his mother and moved on.

His eye caught sight of a bushy plant covered in red berries. Samuel recognized it as a yew tree. Charlotte taught him that the red berries were poisonous, but the Druids held the yew as a sacred tree because of its longevity and ability to regenerate. Where its branches touched the ground, it could grow new trunks. Despite the red berries, the tree radiated a blue hue. A hum resonated from the toxic needles. This tree held the energy of death, as well as regeneration. Out of respect, he asked permission before taking the parchment from between its branches. He unzipped his backpack and pulled out a cushion, which he placed on a nearby stone, and sat down. The text glowed on its own, making it easy to read.

The Genealogist
Yew: Reincarnation & Rebirth

I, Belinda Washington, am a soul family genealogist. My company is called *Beyond*, and I help people see past the limitations of only looking at their current lifetime. I devised a proprietary method of getting a soul sample to derive past life information. This differs from the DNA results that connect you with your earthly blood relations. My clients are believers in reincarnation, puzzled by why they would choose to be in this lifetime with abusive parents, controlling spouses, or toxic siblings that tormented them.

The past life family tree spans many lifetimes, cultures, and time periods. It's fascinating to see one person traveling through various lives in diverse skins, beliefs, and genders. With the knowledge of these experiences and the realization that over centuries we've tried on many personas, any semblance of intolerance or racism vanishes.

Even after doing my own earthly DNA, I found that being a woman of color also included a mix of various colors and cultures in my lineage. That's when it made me curious as to my total experience over many lifetimes. Why, when I visited the Amalfi Coast in Italy for the first time, did sadness fill me upon leaving to the point of tears? There was no ancestral linkage to

Italy in my earthly DNA, but in one lifetime, that area was my home, according to the soul journey results.

My blood family wasn't interested in participating; they saw no reason to understand who they were in a past life, let alone in this one. To me, it boxed them into a limited self-identity. But they don't hold the same beliefs as I do. I've always been captivated by a belief in reincarnation. Guided meditations only got me so far in seeing into other lives. I wanted validation and expanded knowledge of who I was in other lifetimes. The familiar shell I occupied seemed limited in the broader scheme of the Universe.

There were many things I understood in the present that had no connection to anything I'd experienced in my current lifetime. My love of Middle Eastern food, certain fringed garments reminiscent of Indigenous American culture that was comfortable and looked great on me, and an affiliation with Japanese art and architecture. When my soul journey results came back, all these elements were present and more. These components were disparate and odd if looked at purely from direct experience in this life. Or from what is now called cultural appropriation. But it doesn't seem that way when I've spent at least one, sometimes more, lifetimes in these ethnicities. It's more like an assimilation and honoring of the culture.

Beyond my soul's experiences, I get to see where it connects to others and how we related to one another in a past life. Most of my closest friends were with me in other lifetimes. We chose to come back together. They also submitted themselves to the soul journey process so we could get a complete picture of our time together and try to remember. It was easier when we all understood our past lives and how they connected to one another.

As for our earthly families, we recognized their role was to learn from us or for them to teach us certain lessons, such as tolerance, overcoming pain, love, self-worth, and letting go.

One day, a client, Jane, called saying she wanted to do a soul journey report on her brother, Patrick. They had an excruciatingly difficult relationship. It was hard for her to be around him. He exhibited cold, extroverted behavior toward her. He had good social skills because he'd learned to project a positive self-image with the people who could move him up the social and career ladder. As a self-centered narcissist, he took things too personally. There was a hunger for power and a need to be in charge. His skills at getting what he wanted through manipulation left emotional scars on those who cared about him, especially his immediate family. Patrick was good at guilt-tripping people. He withheld love or affection and he had a malicious sense of humor. It was always hurtful, with jokes that targeted others' self-esteem. He exploited others' pain, so his sense of superiority was second nature to him.

Jane tried figuring out what lessons or teachings were inherent in their current lifetime together, to no avail. She worried about his karma and how he'd pay for his behavior. She believed in the balancing force of the Universe that harmonized positive and negative energy. It wasn't up to her to punish Patrick for his inconsiderate and toxic behavior. Whether in this life or the next, she believed her brother would pay the price in whatever fate the Universe determined was best in this incarnation or the next. Wondering if the problem stemmed from a past life, she requested my services. The issue was that her brother needed to give permission and provide a soul sample to look into his past lives.

To convince Patrick of the value of this information, Jane told him of her concern. Honesty protects from karmic backlash, and she wanted to make sure she had integrity in influencing him rather than using his approach of manipulation. He didn't believe her. Switching tactics, she argued it would benefit him to acquire true power. What he thought she meant was power over others. Her intended meaning was power over himself. It worked.

When I received the soul family results, I was shocked to see that they had been husband and wife three lifetimes ago and kept coming back together in various types of relationships to overcome the pain and work through what they experienced ever since. While the first lifetime together was as a married couple, the next was father and daughter, and the incarnation before the current one was employer and employee. In all of them, Patrick's role was the abusive one in control of Jane's circumstances.

Part of journeying together is the karmic agreement between the players. With Patrick playing essentially the same character, it seemed his purpose was to push Jane into setting boundaries and overcoming her lack of self-worth. Despite the irony of an abuser helping the victim find greater value in themselves, it made sense. Jane succumbed to Patrick's behavior in each lifetime. She focused more on how difficult he was instead of understanding that the agreement expected her to set boundaries and separate herself from the situation. It was an interaction she had set up for herself before she was reborn into the next lifetime, taking him with her.

My services include karmic coaching on the results, helping the client understand how to unravel the relationships built over many incarnations and take responsibility for lessons they determined for themselves. The light of recognition shone in her eyes. This wasn't about fixing Patrick, but managing her reaction to him and vowing not to continue this dance of power. Just as her intention was to give him power over himself, it was really about standing in her own power. At that moment, the agreement was fulfilled, the cycle broken, and she began making choices based on her highest good. The next time I saw her, she sparkled.

Patrick asked about the results and how he could use them. When he saw he was there to show Jane her strength, he realized why he had seen her as weak all this time. We delved further into his lifetimes and uncovered that at one point he was the one being abused. It made him think the abuser had the power that he wanted, and so became an abuser himself. His life shifted after our discussion about karma. Patrick decided to change his fate in the present lifetime by helping those trying to heal from abuse. His power in that field rose to unexpected heights with television appearances, packed auditoriums at his speaking engagements, bestselling books, and a popular podcast.

Through my work with others and analysis of my soul journey, I learned not to judge based on appearance. There are many underlying layers to a person, and understanding how we are all connected can bring us together in astonishing ways.

Samuel's Questioning

Belinda's story changed the way Samuel thought of every relationship he ever had. If he'd chosen the people in his life, including his mother, that put a unique spin on how he experienced them. They were teachers, all, helping him move forward in his life in mysterious ways. Just like this forest and the tree spirits within it, his sense of why Charlotte required certain things of him after her death was clearer. He was instinctively moving toward something. With each tree he visited and each story they shared, his view of the world dramatically shifted.

How many lives had he experienced? He tended toward certain inexplicable preferences in food, music, and art that made him seek them out with no prior exposure and no direct knowledge. An idea would pop into his mind and he'd pursue it. What was the origin of these thoughts? Could it come from past incarnations? The idea intrigued him enough to seek ways in which he could explore previous lives.

Samuel's tendency toward pessimism gave way to seeing that perspective colored his life and his choices. Change was up to him. Samuel could temper his tendency to keep to himself by opening himself up to a new way of being.

He looked up at the moon and the glowing trees around him. Off to the right, movement caught his eye. The hooded figure floated between the trees. With each pass, the entity touched a branch, increasing the light that shined from it. Understanding replaced the sense of foreboding he experienced before. It still lacked a human essence, but it demonstrated benevolence in its purpose.

Samuel followed it and watched as it touched Charlotte's sycamore, causing a powerful growth spurt, and giving him hope that he'd soon get to read his mother's story. The figure moved deeper into the dark woods and disappeared.

A deep breath in filled his senses with loam and damp woods. Crickets chirped, filling the air with natural magic. He silently asked the forest to show him the next tree spirit. A bright pink glow pulsed to his left, and he made his way over to the largest black walnut tree he'd ever seen. It looked to be about fifty feet in height and grew straight and tall in the dense forest. Charlotte told him that those who prized its wood made off with black walnut trees in the dead of night. Gently touching the trunk, it shared its book with Samuel, who made himself comfortable as the story unfolded.

The Metaphysician
Black Walnut: Discernment & Wisdom

I'm Bertram Magnus, professor emeritus of metaphysics at the University of Heraclitus. They named the university after the ancient Greek philosopher who believed in cyclical change, where life transforms into death and repeats indefinitely. I came here as a young instructor who subscribed to the Heraclitus belief system. I've spent my career here joyfully pondering, discussing, studying, and writing about the underlying features of reality and the nature of being.

As part of my retirement, I retained my one-bedroom apartment on campus and was given space in the philosophy building to meet with students and to lecture. Even in my sixties, my talks are well-attended. The topics are as relevant as they've ever been. Many of my students are interested in the nature of consciousness and the idea of a universal mind holding all wisdom. It is from this fount we tap ancient and modern knowledge and apply it to today's problems.

A particularly enthusiastic student named Gabriel approached me in the quad on my way home. He wanted to know how we can know ourselves if the self was constantly changing. The search for self and our identity occurs in every stage of life. I shared that with each change, the self transforms, as does the way we look at our lives. It's not just the self that changes, but also the circumstances we find ourselves in. The world changes, society shifts, ideas and beliefs transmute, and we find the need to alter ourselves accordingly, otherwise we're unable to function to our highest potential.

He sat with this idea for a moment and then summed up that change necessitates further change.

I confirmed the accuracy of his statement.

Then he asked if others were required to change if he transformed.

There is no requirement for others to change, as we are each on our own path. Each person holds sovereignty over themselves and is not obligated to change was my answer.

Gabriel informed me he was the first in his family to attend an institute of higher learning and many of his relatives resisted the idea. They had come to conclusions about him that were untrue. He sadly stated that their perception of him changed merely because of his opportunity to study, insisting he was the same person he'd always been.

I asked if he'd changed since coming here and taking classes; if his perspective had changed regarding himself and the world.

The young man confirmed that it had, in unexpected and wonderful ways, but that he didn't see his family as lesser because he was learning. He saw them unchanged, their lives the same as they'd always been, doing the same routine daily. Gabriel depended on their consistency, support, and encouragement to continue elevating himself.

I asked him about his family's opportunity to advance. Should you expect them to play the same role they always have because you need them to do so for your benefit? Have they expressed their hopes and dreams of bettering themselves and their circumstances?

Gabriel fell silent.

I continued. Do you believe you're the only one whose fate deserves change? Are you the arrogant student your family observes you to be? It is extremely difficult to view ourselves objectively. Look at your identity from the core of your being to separate self-awareness from who others observe you to be.

Gabriel froze. I took this to mean he had a profound revelation.

I thought about my own self-image. Are there multiple realities and am I different in each projecting reality onto the external world? Had I modified my reality based on emotional, mental, physical, or spiritual aspects? Am I creating my world using the divine mind and using imagination to create what I want?

I heard a distant beeping noise and a prick in my arm. My legs were stiff, and I was a bit cold. An extended amount of time outside with Gabriel had given me a chill. And then a sharp pain in my chest shocked me out of the quad and into the hospital room where I'd been for a month, creating, dreaming, imagining.

Samuel's Creating Reality

The story shook Samuel to the core. Was he really in this glowing forest reading Bertram's story? It might mean that he can create any reality he wanted through imagination and shifting his perspective. No longer angry at Charlotte for forcing him into this magical forest, he assessed himself at the soul level, as Bertram suggested, sensing his feelings, separating himself from the external world.

The luminescence of the surrounding trees made Samuel question if it was real or something he imagined. Could his senses be trusted? He closed his eyes, experienced the sensation of his sneakers sinking into the moist soil, and asked to be shown the truth. As he opened his eyes, the same lights surrounded him, the trees whispered secrets, and the vibration of dense, unseen life in the forest cemetery made his skin prickle. Maybe this was the truth unseen by most and certainly not seen by Samuel until now.

He stood for another moment, aware of every sensation surrounding him, then drove home to sleep on the stories the trees had shared with him.

The dark forest visit agreed with him, so he returned at the same time the following night. The moon was fuller and brighter. Humidity thickened the air and made the glowing bubbles of light more intense. He found himself standing before an impressively tall spruce tree shining bright yellow from between its densely needled branches, heavy with long, brown cones waiting to release their seeds. Each cone radiated sky blue light. The combination evoked a sense of inspiration and tranquility in Samuel, as if he were on the verge of conjuring something magical for the betterment of others.

Charlotte had spoken to him about the lore of spruce trees, how their evergreen quality made them symbols of longevity and connection to the Divine. For practical use, they were the choice of makers of musical instruments such as violins and pianos for the wood's beautiful tone.

Samuel reached between the thick needles and pulled out a book shaped like a cello. It vibrated in his palm, making him eager to read the story it held.

The Musician

Spruce: Resilience & Connection to the Divine

My name was Eli James, a virtuoso able to play any instrument I picked up from an early age. My abilities astounded people, but I was simply using my gift to sense the energy of the instrument and pull out the music waiting to be released. Whether a piano, woodwind, or string instrument, it spoke to me and moved my hands along its playing surface. The process was completely natural, and I wondered why everyone couldn't do it.

When it happened, I found myself in another world where everything comprised tone and vibration. It ran through my body, filling every bone and pore. I heard what the instrument wanted me to play. Every note held inside the wood and metal came forward, asking for representation. The music waiting there was apparent and inherent to the instrument. Sometimes, the energies of the instrument's creator expressed themselves, adding a powerful undercurrent to the lighter notes of the wood.

Requests to teach students who held promise came frequently, but how could I share my very personal process and the way my senses tuned to the instrument itself? Those who experienced rejection spread the word that I didn't desire competition. But that was not the case. There was no way to compete with something that came naturally, so I encouraged them to develop their own methods. They took my suggestion with the same disdain as my refusal to teach.

I began opening concerts by telling the audience of my musical journey that this ability to hear the desires of the instruments I played came without prompting. It came naturally with music but with nothing else. It was my only talent, and there was no way to prove this to be the case.

One day, an audience member tested my claim. He approached the stage with an unusual instrument he designed. There was no other in the world. It was oddly shaped, somewhat like a cello, with two necks, one resembling that used on a violin and the other like a guitar. A keyboard sat below the strings. He had made each piece from different types of wood. When he handed it to me, the energy overwhelmed my senses with a mixture of natural components and his own chaotic notions.

He had no name for this instrument, no one had ever played it, but once in my hands, it seemed like a generator, pushing forward its agenda with strange power. I closed my eyes, and it took me. Planets came into view through the colorful gases of the universe. Stars, the moon, and foreign galaxies appeared as my hands flowed over strings and keys. I traveled back in time to observe ancient rituals and leaped forward to witness civilization dwelling in skyscrapers suspended in the air. As I plucked the strings, it evoked visions of primordial forests and underground dwellings. I played until my fingers were numb and my mind became blank.

When I opened my eyes, the audience sat dumbfounded. I was in a sort of shock from what I'd seen while I played the unnamed instrument. A blast of wind had blown their hair into disarray. Many held their heads in what looked like confusion or pain. Silence fell over the audience when they normally would give a standing ovation. The inventor of the instrument looked at me with wide eyes, his jaw moving up and down without sound. I noticed moisture on my hands and discovered blood on my fingertips. My ears buzzed. The smell of sweat, my own and the audience's, permeated the room. My clothes and hair were damp. Tears in my pant leg where I held the instrument let in warm air. The room temperature had increased significantly as I played.

What had I unleashed from this odd instrument? Not even the inventor expected these results.

Murmurs among the audience spread and grew louder. I heard them ask one another what they had just seen and heard. Did the person next to them see the planets and fly through space? What about the ancient forest with trees so big they couldn't have been real? That's when I realized what I'd done; carried the audience along with me. It was music of the ages, of history, of nature, and of the future. There was no chronology, images without order.

The instrument's inventor held up an electronic device, yelling he'd recorded the music. I looked over to my sound engineers, who nodded, letting me know they captured the wild musical ride, as well. When played back, would the recording take listeners on the same journey as the live concert? Would they even want to go on a trip like that again? I wasn't sure I wanted to.

Staggering off stage, I struggled to get to my manager, who was waiting with a glass of water. I chugged it down and ran a hand through my hair, which stood straight up, to smooth it. I asked her what happened. She shook her head and told me she wasn't sure, but now that she's coming out of the stupor the music put her in, she felt more enlightened somehow.

She asked what I planned to do with the strange instrument, which I hadn't realized was still in my left hand. With a shrug, I wondered why the inventor hadn't come after me. The theater manager came over to let us know people weren't leaving. They still sat in the audience without the usual applause, calling me for an encore. I overheard some of them saying their back pain was gone or that their hearing had improved; they could hear whispers from across the room, as could I. This made me feel better about the effect the instrument had had on everyone, including me.

The feeling slowly returned to my fingers, and I rested the weird instrument on a guitar stand. A little steadier on my feet, I walked back onto the stage. People stood and clapped and yelled. The inventor was still at the foot of the stage. I invited him to come up and join me. The applause grew thunderous, and we both took a bow and walked behind the curtain.

We collapsed into upholstered chairs in my dressing room. A deep conversation ensued about the making of the instrument, its wood, and its shape. The wood had come from a secret forest in the wilds of Germany, fallen tree trunks and branches of unknown species were used to create the instrument. Although the inventor was a musician of some renown himself, attempts to play his creation produced weak and unimaginative sounds. The resonance potential of the wood and the shape had no bearing on the sound quality until I played it using my unusual method. He gifted me the one-of-a-kind instrument and said his hands were the tools being guided to make it for me.

His experience and understanding of how I brought his invention to life validated what I had been saying all along about why I couldn't teach my method. Journalists reported the unexpected results of the preternatural music that came from the unique instrument. Recordings of the extraordinary concert earned the two of us millions. Acousticians analyzed the frequencies of the music and determined they had no equal. Medical professionals worked to understand the healing powers of the odd music and its broad effects on health and wellbeing.

Concerts featuring the instrument, which came to be known as Enigma, put it last on the program prefaced with a warning. Despite all the information available about Enigma, the direct experience still surprised audiences. I grew to call each piece that came forth *Trips*. In fact, that was the name of the first album recorded using Enigma. Each trip took me and listeners on a healing journey different from the last one. To reproduce the same song was an impossible task, hence the variation in the trip. Together, we traveled through galaxies and timelines, geographies containing ancient buildings and cultures, and ultimately, we traveled deep within ourselves. Along the way, we spread uplifting energies to the places we visited, connected to universal consciousness, and ultimately healed ourselves.

Samuel's Transformational Frequencies

Samuel could feel the truth in James's story about the healing power of music, especially when a shared experience lifts everyone. The idea that certain frequencies could overcome illness or injury appealed to him. Never having been musical himself, he couldn't imagine composing or playing the notes, but held hope that one day scientists would find the magical frequencies to heal. He wished he could listen to the Enigma recordings and travel with James.

In the meantime, the music of chirping crickets, rubbing their wings together at an angle that creates a resonating chamber like the body of a violin, nocturnal bird calls, and mammals scratching for food, filled his ears and relaxed his body. The night was cooler than usual and the moon was full, adding to the mystical feeling of these spirit-filled woods.

He found that two stories a night were his limit, so he scanned the area to find his second. A blue and green glow attracted him to a tree about fifty yards from where he stood. As Samuel got closer, he saw it was a Ginkgo Biloba tree. He easily recognized its fan-shaped leaves and remembered his mother keeping bottles of its extract to improve her blood flow and memory.

The book the tree released into his hands was thicker than the others. He flipped through and found it was the life book of an author. It contained not only her autobiography, but some of her short stories and novels as well. Samuel's mother encouraged her son to write about what he felt and what he learned. To read this author's story could give him insight into the process of writing. He sat on his blanket and opened the spirit book to her personal story.

The Author

Ginkgo Biloba: Hope, Peace, & Love

Andrea Springs is my real name, but my pen name is Linda Hopewell. Call me what you feel relates to how you think of me after reading about my writing journey. It's different for every writer, their process, their subject matter, and their writing voice. The writing draws readers by how it makes them feel or what they learn. Some readers want to escape from reality, others want to go deeper into history or how characters deal with pain, escaping what traps them. Whatever their reasons, the author hopes their work strikes a chord with them on some level. When an author writes, they share a part of themselves and what they care about.

The effort required to produce a published manuscript takes perseverance, dedication, and love. Some money may come from the book, but most times not. It's up to the author to provide what readers want and readers need to spread the word about books they enjoy. They are the author's many loves, the ones who connect with what the writer tries to say in a way that speaks to them.

For me, the writing feels right when I channel the text. It comes through me from somewhere in the universe, flowing onto the page. Peace comes when this happens; the zone is a calm place, allowing me to travel through the story and bring it to life for readers. When you engage with my work, we share our energies and connect across time and space.

I wrote romance novels about unrequited love and unconventional couplings. Most writers hope our books reach far and wide. Mine didn't reach as far as Dickens and didn't have the staying power of Austen or the Bronte sisters, but I wrote what I liked and those who liked my writing voice stayed with me for each publication. My work had a small but loyal following.

One day a man, I'll call him Jack to keep him anonymous, knocked on my door and asked me to write the story of the death of his wife, Adelaide. Not knowing him, I walked outside and closed the door behind me.

He described her as a star that fell from the sky to serve humanity and couldn't decide what to focus on. She worked hard to benefit others until she became ill and knew her time was ending. It sounded like a story about good deeds and how Adelaide's work was a godsend for so many. There might be a small market for that type of book, but mostly, my readers look for romance, conflict, and betrayal. Stories about kindness don't stimulate the public.

And then he dropped the bomb. He never loved Adelaide. He betrayed his wife with another woman, and Adelaide knew instinctively that he wanted to leave but didn't want to hurt her. A pause. And how he poisoned her drink so that she died.

There it was; all three elements in one horrific story wrapped around a confession to murder. Do I write the story or call the police? Is the desire for success worth giving credence to this killer?

Jack continued. The woman with whom he had the affair discovered he'd killed Adelaide and left him. She was afraid for her own life. What would stop Jack from doing the same to her once he grew tired of the relationship?

I asked Jack what he'd get out of me writing his story? What motivated him? The money? There was no guarantee of how many sales we'd have. Would my readers rebel if I gave them something different from what they expected? Was this an opportunity to change the course of my career and reach a broader audience? Besides, my publisher would have to accept the manuscript as a viable project; legal papers needed signing.

Silence. Then, he said it was to rid himself of the guilt. I could have the story to write as fiction and owed him nothing but time to hear the full story, his confession. My publisher gave the go-ahead, and we met regularly, his story pouring out of him as though he removed a plug from a dam. Each meeting lasted three or four hours; I wrote for as long after he left. Weeks went by until the story was complete. It went beyond the outline he told me when we first met.

The story had a strange effect on me; I felt heavy, the density of his guilt and pain weighing on me as though it were my own. I wondered how true crime authors managed the cruelty they faced when writing about the facts of the case. My usual storyline made me feel light and flowing with the relationships within the story, even when there was a loss.

The effect it had on me put that leaden energy into the writing and onto whoever read it. How would they experience my work? Integrity was utmost, giving readers what they desired and setting expectations for what they were about to open themselves up to.

At last, the manuscript was complete. Grateful for the ordeal to be over, I reluctantly turned it in to my publisher. The reception surprised me. He predicted a bestseller from the sensitively written, heinous story of a man's guilt and his crimes against the innocent. Was it possible I had absorbed the pain of the story to take it away from the readers' experience and leave them with understanding and compassion? Had I translated his confession to make my audience see his side and not condemn him as he chastised himself?

Perhaps my role in this was to create objectivity, exonerate the man to a degree, and help him shed the guilt he felt. Applying his story to the page without judgment allowed me to tell the story and increase understanding of human nature. The book became popular, giving me the money to work on other projects, while readers sought books with my pen name, making them bestsellers.

For Jack, his story released in a form that showed him a new perspective on his actions, he moved forward with a renewed conviction for acting in the best interest of others as Adelaide would have wanted him to.

As for me, my writing shifted in unexpected ways. Balanced storytelling showed readers both sides of the characters, a blend of motivations, and letting them decide the true nature of their actions, as we do in real life. My stories brought hope for exoneration, peace in accepting what's been done, and love toward those who need it.

Samuel's Sharing

Samuel envied the author and the musician, knowing what their purpose was and how to express it. What was his purpose? When Charlotte was alive, his purpose was to manage her affairs. Now, despite being lost in the forest of options, the spirits somehow guided him toward something still unknown.

Samuel thought about the author's ordeal and how much of herself she invested into the story. Her investment and concern for her readers struck him in the heart. Could he write in such a way to benefit others? Like the stories the tree spirits shared with him, they benefited him and his own life. Was he allowed to share them? Should he write them down? He'd wait and see. His mother's tree was still to come, so he'd wait for what she had to reveal to him before deciding.

For now, he wanted his comfortable bed, so he packed up and headed home.

Sticking with his evening ritual, Samuel returned to the cemetery after dark. He had grown to love the glowing trees and the potent life force emanating from them. With anticipation for another life-changing story, he made his way through the main gate and headed towards an area of the cemetery he hadn't explored before. He picked his way through tall grass and mushy earth and came upon a beautiful circle of wildflowers planted around a crape myrtle loaded with hot pink blooms, an orange glow radiated around the trunk and along the branches. Purple phlox, orange asters, and white foxglove mixed with maidenhair and royal fern decorated the space, completed by a concrete ornamental bench. No other trees had flowers planted around them.

The flowers had a shine all their own, different from the tree; the phlox with its sweet scent glowed with sparkles of white, the foxglove had a bitter scent and shone with tiny flecks of gold, and the asters had no fragrance until Samuel picked one and crushed it between his fingers, releasing a balsam-like scent and speckles of silver. Dense fern radiated green and white light, feeding Samuel with energy he didn't know he needed.

Sitting on the bench revitalized him and washed him in peace. It felt like anything was possible and he was ready for whatever change was coming and welcomed the shifts he'd already experienced. The book, bound by a green cover that looked like a large leaf, suddenly appeared on the bench next to him. He picked it up gently, feeling the silky finish, and reverently opened the book.

The Gardener

Crape Myrtle: Love, Balance, & Change

I, Rose Flores, hope you're enjoying my little garden. Feeling my time was ending, I worked to plan and plant the flowers and the ferns before my tree received my cremains. The grave digger received specific instructions so he wouldn't disrupt my design.

My botanical education began as a child, with Grandma giving me a tour of her extensive garden. Every season, something new bloomed. She passed her skill down to me. The genetic component jumped over my mother and came directly to me. My certification as a master gardener made me credible when others hired me to manage their outdoor projects.

Customers dubbed how I did my work as the *Flores Touch*, bringing back plants thought to be past their time and designing gardens, so they never needed pesticides to flourish. Hummingbirds, butterflies, and bees thrived in the gardens I planted. To sit amidst the plants and the pollinators brought balance to the heart and mind and created a deep connection to nature.

The awards I received didn't hold a candle to the way people felt when they experienced my work. That was the true reward. Working with plants and being outside lifted me higher still. It was why Spirit put me on this earth. Prayers said in my gardens rose higher and worked faster than in any other place. Those who did so felt the flow of Spirit within and around them and saw the humor in things that bothered others. They underwent a profound metamorphosis in preparation for any eventuality, being led down the right path and overcoming obstacles with grace in times of difficulty. My gardens made it possible to have the energy to rise above hardship.

Thoughts floated gently into mind, walking along flagstone pathways through flowers bursting with color, creating the next phase of life. The gardens strengthened folks so they could take the next step in manifesting their desires. Miracles unfolded as reality changed before their eyes, bestowing upon them their dearest dreams.

I was working in a public garden, wearing soil-caked gardening gloves and planting petunias, when a man approached me. His hair was in disarray, his business suit rumpled, and his eyes were red and puffy. With a clenched jaw, he asked if I was the master gardener who designed his friend's garden. I rose, removed my gloves, and confirmed I was. His name was Harvey, and he needed my services as soon as possible, for he was at a crossroads, abandoned by friends and family, and divided as to his path. It was clear his focus was building wealth, and that relationships were temporary, mere stepping stones to create money. There was nothing more important in the world for him.

I let him speak, feeling the pain of his chosen path, marked with regret, and looking for a quick remedy for his plight. He told me his neighbor seemed happier than she'd ever been since I installed her garden. That's how he wanted to feel. Could I come this afternoon to design a garden for him?

The word *healing* came into my mind. He needed a garden to heal him, but also a direction that remedied his loneliness. This man needed love. My secret ingredient in the garden was exactly that, for love brought everything together and raised the energy of the environment. I let him lead me to his home, which was as rundown as he was. He had money but no time to care for his house. With overgrown grass, the formerly white picket fence covered in peeling paint, and the muddy yard in complete disorder, I got right to work.

I walked the property, envisioning which plants brought higher spiritual vibrations, felt where they needed to be placed, and saw the colors to bring joy. My instructions to him included hiring someone to mow the grass in the front and back and to paint the fence, which he did. With Harvey's help, we removed old buckets, broken statuary, and other trash from the yard, talking all the while. He still wore his suit, so I suggested he change into gardening clothes. When he came out wearing jeans and a T-shirt, Harvey looked more relaxed than before.

We got into my pickup truck and drove to the garden store, where we selected the flowers and trees for the design. Pavers were next, a bench, and a birdbath. When we arrived back at his house, the hired hand had mowed the grass and a painter was working on the fence. Harvey and I brought everything to the back, along with my tools. It was late in the day, so we set a time to start bright and early the next morning.

The drawing I did that night gave him paths to stroll down, trees to shade him, and places to sit. Harvey came out of the house to greet me, eyes sparkling, comfortable in work clothes. His excitement over the plan warmed me, and we got to work. At one point, he left to go inside and brought us lemonade to enjoy on a folding table, where we could assess the work done so far. He gazed across the space and smiled.

I think he enjoyed the planting most, getting his hands in the soil, gently removing the flowers from their pots, and lovingly covering their roots with dirt. He had stamina for planting. I watched his energy grow with each segment of ground we completed. He got the painter to help us install the flagstone path and to dig the bigger holes for the trees. As the sun set, the garden breathed in the twilight air. Harvey leaned against the shovel, looking pleased with what he'd created.

I turned on the sprinklers and let the garden settle in. Out front, the entire house looked refreshed, with a mown lawn and a bright white picket fence. Harvey stood at the back gate waving to me, saying he looked forward to my checking in with him in a few days.

Upon my return, there was a beautiful woman sitting at an ornate bistro set across from Harvey. He rose and greeted me, and then introduced me to his wife, Arlene. She complimented me on the garden, saying it brought life back to both the house and to Harvey. I gave her husband all the credit, for he jumped into the project with gusto and put lots of love into creating this paradise. Seated once again, Harvey reached for Arlene's hand and squeezed it affectionately. My stroll through the garden showed it was thriving, along with Harvey. All they both needed was love and a balanced approach to living.

Samuel's Directing Love

To have a place or person in which to direct love was important for living a full life. Money alone didn't give Harvey what he truly needed; to have an intimate relationship with first his garden and have it lead to a reunion with his estranged wife filled the need of his soul. Samuel thought of his mother and missed their relationship. He knew he'd have to develop friendships locally. Once he finished meeting his new tree spirit friends, he'd work on that.

Samuel also envisioned a garden similar to the design Rose made for Harvey at his own cottage. He looked forward to researching plants, bloom times, and sunlight requirements. Those that are deer resistant would be ideal, since there was a large population roaming area. He might even make some friends in the gardening groups nearby.

A majestic rowan tree pulled him from visions of his beautiful garden. Loaded with red berries, its energy was also red, shining around the trunk and up into the branches. Revered for their protection qualities, the rowan warded off witchcraft and enchantment. It also protected the spirits of the dead, so its presence in this cemetery was perfect. Samuel expected to find more as he explored.

He reached under the full canopy between the branches, heavily laden with berries, and found the book written by this tree spirit. He wondered how the spirit chose which story to share or if the story changed depending on who was reading. That was something to test going forward, for he realized he'd spend years roaming this forest and getting to know its residents.

The Detective

Rowan: Protection Against Witchcraft and Enchantment & Protection for the Spirits of the Dead

My name was Erin Clark. I lived in the sleepy town of Rowan, Pennsylvania. Our town got its name from the giant Rowan tree that stood in the center of town, along with many others privately planted by the residents on their property. As a tree of protection, it was bad luck to cut one down, so people treated them with respect. People believed strongly in this legend and swore that the town's safety depended on them. Their superstitions ran deep; the residents of Rowan respected their trees and abided by their superstitions.

Naturally curious, I watch people and make note of their behavior. My intention is to ensure protection of the local folks, making sure the actions of visitors and residents don't do harm. So, I investigate. I uncover things not apparent to others that could harm them, especially those who didn't take the time to plant a rowan tree on their property. Those with rowan trees on their property were unaffected by enchantments spurred on by jealousy, revenge, or other strong negative emotions. For those without this protective tree, I brought a sapling as a gift to ward off dark intentions.

It was my habit to walk through town and along the backstreets at all hours of the day and night to stay aware of activity or something brewing. One night, as the cool wind rustled the rowan's branches, I noticed a boy peeking out from behind the tree. I waved at him, and he ducked behind the trunk, so I walked around behind the tree, and he was gone. He appeared down the road a few shops down, signaling me to follow him.

Knowing that kids are very observant, he piqued my curiosity, so I followed. His clothes were outdated and his image wavered in the breeze. The boy pointed at a doorway I had never seen before. The windows on either side were dark, and the door itself was metal, dinged top to bottom with thin, inch-wide dents. I ran my hand over them, silver metal showing through where black paint crumbled off. The door hummed with energy and heat. I turned to the boy, but he was gone.

I tried the knob, and it turned. Out of the darkness, heat and the smell of charred wood washed over me. I stood to the side, letting the warmth out into the cool night before going in. A switch was inside to the left of the door. I flicked it up. A bare bulb illuminated the room, showcasing scorched walls, a tattered sofa, a blackened upholstered chair, seared furniture and wood flooring, burned bones, slips of paper with a letter or two remaining unburnt, and other odds and ends scattered across the floor.

What was this place? I've lived here all my life and never knew this existed.

The boy appeared across the room and pointed to a spot on the wall. There was a rectangle cut with a small handle attached. I pulled it open to find a logbook with the names of women currently living in town, alongside a column labeled *wishes*, all written in the same hand, which included money, children, a husband, a house, health, and the desire to be beautiful. The last column had the title "wish granted" and a date; its last entry occurring only a week ago.

I thought about the women on the page. I knew most of them. They attained what they wanted. How did their wishes come true and who was keeping track?

I looked over at the boy, who put his finger to his mouth, signaling not to tell anyone, and then burst into flames.

The smell overwhelmed me, so I took the logbook and left, closing the door behind me. I heard a whooshing sound, and the door disappeared.

Clinging to the book, I decided to visit each woman's house to see how their wishes affected them. My investigation started that night. As I walked past their homes, I noticed one thing was consistently true: there were no rowan trees on their properties. A few of the women had cut down their rowans, and only the stump remained. It made me wonder who else had cut down their protective rowan tree.

In the morning, I began with the most recent wish fulfilled, a husband, and knocked on her door. A man answered. Knowing him to be the husband of another woman in town, I asked if he was visiting here and if the lady of the house was home. He said he'd remarried and lived there now and, no; she wasn't home but at work, her very first job at forty years old, having lived comfortably off her inheritance until their marriage had depleted it.

My finger ran down the wish list and found his ex-wife's name. She had asked for money, which she got in the divorce settlement, along with the house. When I visited her, I discovered she was now single and not handling it well.

Next stop was the woman who wanted beauty. I remembered her as someone very grounded and naturally attractive, with men flocking around her. When she opened the door, she was in full makeup, a pretty dress, and her hair done in an up-do. It looked like she had a facelift, with skin tight and eyes stretched, no longer looking like the lovely woman I knew. The change made her appear high maintenance, so none of the men in town came calling. Her down-turned mouth showed her sadness.

When I knocked on the door of the woman who wished for a child, I heard a baby screaming. She came to the door, hair sticking up, baby food and vomit on her shirt, smelling like she needed a shower. I knew her as a successful business owner, always put together and smiling. Now, her life was upside down, having had to give up her business with no time to manage it.

The woman who desired health had been a cancer patient. She gained health through a mastectomy with hopes it would not spread. She wanted full restoration as she was prior to surgery. I asked how she had been granted her wish. She said someone had sworn her to secrecy.

My guess was whoever wrote in the logbook was the one who helped them fulfill their desires, but at a high price. There are two sides to every desire, and this wizard, or whatever he was, made out the best and the women all lost something meaningful to them. Remembering the charred contents of the strange room, they likely provided more to their grantor than they bargained for.

I set out in search of this shyster while simultaneously looking for samples of handwriting and researching residents who arrived shortly before the logbook started. I wasn't sure what uncovering him would do to improve these women's lives or at least restore their lives, but first I had to find him.

The municipal building in the county seat held public records such as deeds and mortgages to houses purchased in Rowan. I found no record within the timeframe I looked for. The person might rent rather than own, so I asked around to find out if any new residents were renting in Rowan. Nothing. How had the women found him? I kept thinking it was a male, but I could be wrong, and opened my thoughts to the possibility of a woman.

Then it struck me to walk the two-square miles of Rowan and investigate if anyone had cut down any more trees. I started on the outskirts of town where the woods were thick until I saw a hole in the dense forest where a large rowan tree once stood. I trotted over to it and noticed a small cabin with a man sitting out front. Alarms sounded loudly in my head. I knew this was the culprit.

He wore an eggplant purple colored robe trimmed with symbols embroidered along the edge. He sat looking at me expectantly and waved me over. I stood my ground. He smiled and said he'd been waiting for me; he felt me searching for him. Those who needed his services found him and got what they asked for.

Satisfied with my life overall, my desire was simple; for him to leave our town and restore it to the state in which he'd found it. That included the rowan trees. A look of shock came to his face. It seemed he'd expected me to ask for something for myself. Needing nothing more than I had, there was nothing he could hold over me. With a reluctant wave of his hand, the rowan tree he'd cut down regenerated. He bowed his head and disappeared.

The sack I carried suddenly seemed lighter. I looked inside and the logbook was gone. With a spring in my step, I trotted back to town. As I passed by the houses without rowan trees, I discovered they were there once again, as big and strong as they had been before. The woman who asked for beauty came out of her door wearing jeans and a sweater, looking better than ever with a bright smile lighting her face. Men vied for her attention and walked with her as she did errands. At her shop, the business owner appeared in her display window and waved as she happily arranged her wares. The previously divorced husband and wife looked reconciled as they walked down the sidewalk holding hands. After renewed appreciation of her situation, the heir regained her inheritance and sat on her porch, gently rocking and knitting. Finally, the woman fighting cancer accepted her treatment options, grateful for the medical advancements that lengthened her life.

My desire fulfilled, it came without compromise, for it wasn't for myself that I performed my investigation, but for the wellbeing of others. While it's not recommended to step into another's path, all I requested on their behalf was to put things back the way they were before the wizard meddled in their destiny. Where had he gone, anyway? I hoped banishing him prevented further mischief, but I couldn't know for sure.

What I knew was that with lessons hopefully learned, these women had a chance to reconsider what they thought were greener pastures and find satisfaction in what they had.

With a detective's persistence, my next investigation would be to find out who the boy spirit was who tipped me off to the evil festering in my beloved town of Rowan.

Samuel's Being Present

Another case of *be careful what you wish for* made Samuel focus on the things he had now rather than wanting his former life. He wouldn't give up the experiences he'd had in these woods for anything. Plus, the little house he purchased had grown on him, and he felt peace and comfort there. The one thing that would add an even greater sense of satisfaction was a dog. That would come in time. And it would be the right dog. Did this cemetery allow dogs? There was never anyone but him here anyway, so he didn't think the trees would mind.

It was almost morning, so time to head home. Tomorrow, he'd start with one last tree before checking on his mother's progress.

The next evening, Samuel followed his nose to the scent of pine and found a pine tree soaring above him. The light shining from it was dark green. As an evergreen, it was a symbol of eternal life and protection. Charlotte cleaned with a pine cleanser, saying it balanced emotions and cleared the space of negativity. With that in mind, he retrieved the book of this tree's spirit. The wood binding had pictures of carpentry tools carved into it. It made Samuel think that his guest cottage might make for a good workshop.

The Builder

Pine: Protection for the Construction Crew, Good Luck, & Prosperity for the Building's Future Occupants

My name was Mark Swanson. I built commercial and residential structures across Pennsylvania. During construction, I'd have the crew hoist a pine tree to the top, ensuring their safety and bringing good fortune to future residents of the building. It was a ritual started in 700 A.D. in Scandinavia. I found this in a book and thought it sounded like a good idea. It certainly couldn't hurt.

My favorite projects transformed old buildings for a new purpose. Lots of old dwellings in towns across Pennsylvania needed refurbishing, and I had a passion for it. As the County Seat, the courthouse and other official government buildings were there, along with the people who were part of the daily use of those services.

There was a building in Barnesburg I had my eye on. It was the town's historic prison, slated for demolition. This gave the structure a heavy feeling from all the prisoners' depression, hopelessness, and outrage. This stone masterpiece looked like a castle, with turrets and archways, a magnificent architectural building in need of transformation.

In my mind, I saw the sign above the door: *Pathways to Hope* written in gold neon. My idea was that those who had suffered misfortune would find their way through those doors and experience significant life changes, just like the building would.

So, I purchased it and planted pine trees on the entire perimeter of the property, giving it an immediate lift. A group of spiritual practitioners volunteered to do an energy cleansing of the building, and I took them up on the offer. The pleasant smell of white sage lasted for a week. I hired local contractors to revamp the plumbing, heating, and electrical systems. My regular crew took care of the drywall and painting, and I had experts from county services of all types consult on the best layout to promote healing, motivation, and hope. We turned part of the building into a dormitory with space for one hundred people at a time.

People helped raise money for the project and volunteered their services for the renovation and to provide support to those in need. Drug counselors, psychologists, medical doctors, art therapists, life skills teachers, spiritual counselors, and social workers were on board. We hired three monitors and provided them with small apartments within the building and a stipend to manage the day-to-day issues and traffic.

It was finally opening day. The renovation turned out exactly as I had envisioned it. The mayor came, as did the state's governor, to cut the ribbon and say some inspirational words about the project. I felt my whole body buzzing with excitement as our first residents entered through the archway and went through the onboarding process, getting their identification cards, starting a file that held information about their circumstances and history, and determining goals.

My vision was that the heightened vibration of the building would work its magic on those who entered the facility. It was part of the process. Even those who came as a skeptic would shift into a cooperative stance as they passed beneath the gold neon above the archway, as though sprinkled with magic dust.

Everyone played a part in the success of this endeavor. I was the catalyst, but the people involved pooled their energies and created the success. No one person could have pulled this off; but it took a clear vision to make it happen. The train was rolling, so I took my crew and went on to other jobs, checking back periodically to see how things were going.

I stopped by one day and noticed a man looking desperate, with tattered clothes, a dirty face, and eyes glistening with tears. He hesitated at the steps of *Pathways to Hope*, looking up at the sign and wringing his hands. I went over to him and encouraged him to go through the doorway. He looked at me with a miserable expression, and I nodded. Stepping through the archway, he seemed the same as he was on the sidewalk; odd since I'd seen an instant shift in people from hopeless to hopeful countless times, but not this time.

The man's image wavered, darkened, and then floated down the hall. How had that happened? Was he a former prisoner here? The staff shared they saw spirits here from time to time, but I'd seen nothing to verify their sightings. I followed him past several doorways before I saw one of the spiritual advisors, Clara Bernstein, in her office. When I described what I saw, she nodded her head and said she'd seen that spirit on several occasions in one of the dorm rooms, sometimes in one of the group sessions, always looking around to see if we could help him.

She said we could help him cross over or we could try communicating with him to see what keeps him here. We preferred to do both to help him heal before sending him on his way. The two of us went to the town hall to look at the prison records and photos of inmates to see if we could recognize him and discover more about him. We leafed through binders containing decades' worth of photos of prisoners until we found our mystery man, Cole Hanks.

His ghost was an exact copy of the photo in the binder. The same taut face and forlorn eyes. Arrested and imprisoned for stealing food from a grocery store, Cole, down on his luck, did what he had to in order to survive. Further research showed that he'd lost his job at the local steel plant and desperation set it. He had a family to feed. They sent him to prison for a year. He didn't survive the ordeal. Now Cole's spirit roamed the halls, unsure of what to do next. His family found a way forward and lived back then, although in the present only his son was alive and in his sixties.

Clara suggested we reach out to him psychically. And so, we went to a quiet spot in the building, invited Cole to join us, and let him know that his family made it through and that they knew the sacrifice he made for their welfare. The darkness of his energy brightened a little. Then, Clara said that we thought the punishment for trying to feed his family was harsh and that those in authority should have tried to understand the circumstances instead. The brightness grew. I told him I'd look in on his son and make sure he was fine and that his wife was waiting for him on the other side of the veil.

Cole let a smile light up his face. Beaming, he looked like a healthy, working man, clothes mended and living a happy life. Clara gave him the choice to stay or be with his wife. He nodded once in thanks and waved as he disappeared.

The tragic story of Cole pushed *Pathways of Hope* to a new phase of helping. Even in death, he showed us the way toward another purpose. The organization made sure that those who are hungry get fed and that we find those who don't know about us to ensure they can eat without stealing. We partnered with volunteers from food banks and organizations focused on ending hunger. We contacted Cole's son and told him about his father and what we were doing, so other families wouldn't have to go through that. He became a volunteer and worked tirelessly, ensuring food got to those in need.

My boundless gratitude for the difference *Pathways of Hope* made in the lives of so many lifted me like no other project I'd worked on. People left the building motivated and focused, ready to help others in need. I couldn't ask for anything better. Working with others who had the same vision and connecting to the supportive energy of the Universe lifted those alive and dead. Now I knew the dead carried feelings from life with them that needed to be healed. And the pine trees reflected the positive energy powering the building, and all who came through its doors.

Samuel's Serving Others

Powerful visions. Unexpected inspiration from the past. These are the things that Samuel realized guide us in our next purpose and help us serve others. We're guided every step of the way, yet choose to take the guidance or reject it. Mark the builder could have decided bringing his vision to life was too much trouble, but his enthusiasm for the project sparked others and spoke to their desire to help. Working together is the way to bring large projects to fruition. How could Samuel use these lessons on his own journey?

He'd listen more and in a different way to the messages and guidance he received. Seeking to apply the visions to the big picture of his life and what he stood for, Samuel nodded to himself in understanding the way the Universe supported him all along. This is likely what his mother, and the tree spirits, tried to show him by bringing him here. That, and so much more.

One more story tonight, and then he'd sleep on these latest revelations, his discernment growing by the day and his self-concept expanding beyond what he previously believed possible.

A blackthorn tree stood, radiating burgundy and cobalt blue light. The trunk opened and gave Samuel a scroll marked with an astrology chart at the top, glowing white. It was the chart of the astrologer herself. Open to new insights about himself, Samuel thought getting his chart done would be exciting.

The Astrologer

Blackthorn Tree: Intensity, Passion, & Transformative power

As an astrologer, my work spanning decades, I, Sheila Wiser, sought to bring self-awareness to my clients. This, in turn, transformed and healed their deepest wounds. They'd come hoping for good news in the planetary alignments, wanting to believe that everything was pre-ordained. Part of my calling was to teach them that nothing is written in stone. Free will and the circumstances we create beyond the potential in an astrology chart factors in, as well.

Change is inherent in life and in celestial movement. Stagnation arrests the flow of destiny. What is meant to be doesn't happen when complacency takes over. Clients could take a passive approach to their life, hoping and wishing for their chart to do the work for them. That's not how the Universe works. The natal chart is a map, a quest laid out for you to see your potential. Whether to take action or not is up to the individual.

Most clients want information about relationships, money, health, and career. The real magic in a chart is enhancing self-awareness. But prediction is what they hope for. Admittedly, I see the future, but don't always share it. The chart provides clues that connect and trigger the vision. It comes in images, emotions, and sometimes, scent. At times, I hear messages, as though someone is speaking in my ear. What I share depends on the readiness of the client to hear it.

One day, Eva Honeyman plodded through my door. Something weighed on her slight frame. It was her first astrology reading, and she was excited to hear everything about herself and her future. I explained how celestial bodies continue moving to create new alignments and energetic shifts represented by the planets in signs and houses. These are the cycles of life and the symbols that show us the way forward. First, I showed her the birth or natal chart, the energies she came into this life with and that would guide her until death. Then, the Solar Return chart, which reflects the energies for that birthday year. Finally, in her progressed chart, displaying the positions of the planets on the day she came to see me, along with the transits that affect everyone.

It's essential to understand the energies that press upon us from outside our lives and how our personal lives respond and thrive or crash under the pressure. Eva didn't realize how much information she'd get and how the chart changed with every calculation. She just wanted a simple answer. But there were none. Life is complicated, with vibrational patterns supporting or challenging, lifting or suppressing, coupled with the need to manage these and align with them for the best result.

Clients had to do some work to achieve their aspirations. That's not what most wanted to hear. They wanted the planets to do the work for them and for me to interpret their charts, so they had a clear path to their destiny. But there's a lot of gray area in there, too. Any vision I get is based on what's already taken place, and the future is based on free will and personal choice.

The chart showed Eva coming up on a particularly difficult leg of her journey. She was required to make a choice between two paths, each of which would change her forever. Would she select the option of following someone to a place she wouldn't have gone herself or choose the direction of transformation for her highest good? The choice would take her to a place of her greatest challenge and possible despair, or to a place of contentment, joy, and inner peace.

Eva focused on details when making a decision. This cycle required the big-picture view and how she wanted to feel going forward. Was she satisfied with her life as is, or did she want major changes that took her beyond where she dreamed she could go?

Could I tell her which direction to take? No. I saw each path clearly; one leading to despair, the other to her destiny. Eva hung her head. The smell of frankincense burning on my side table suddenly became cloying. Her internal struggles came forward, her foot tapping the floor and fingers drumming her thighs. Eva told me about a man who promised her the world, but it was his world he wanted to give her. Wealth, excitement, and celebrities were in her future if she was with him. The problem was, her nature didn't support that lifestyle. As an introvert, she preferred quiet time reading or walking in the woods. Famous people and living in luxury weren't priorities for her. But she might regret saying no.

If she didn't go with him, the other trail led to an offer of being a resident teacher at a women's retreat in the mountains. Days filled with quiet contemplation, helping others reach their goals and overcome their fears, all in her favorite wooded environment.

As she spoke of each option, I watched her energy signature change from dark and depressed to lively and bright. I shared this insight with her, comparing it to Saturn, with its purpose being the taskmaster, with discipline, structure, and responsibility as its hallmarks versus Venus, with its focus on beauty and harmony. Her aura reflected these planets and what they represented. At that moment, her decision crystallized. It was easy to see that Venus better represented her natural energy. She loved the man in her life but knew that love would turn to resentment as he lived his life in a way that opposed what she saw for herself. Eva's body relaxed and a smile lit up her face.

The rest of her chart showed ways of maximizing her potential and warnings of stumbling blocks along the way. Eva took notes and underlined the challenges she might face. She rose to leave and gave me a bear hug, thanking me for guiding her to what felt right. It wasn't me, for I'm just the channel, imparting information for my client's highest good.

Samuel's Quiet Knowing

Samuel always thought of astrology as shining light on the unknown, albeit with some skepticism. Sheila's story showed him that validation of what we already feel to be true is part of the process of getting an astrology reading. It's aligning ourselves with our true self and knowing that our body's reaction provides clues as to the best decision.

Samuel felt this now in his cottage. His body relaxed when he walked through the door. He smiled easier than he ever had before. Even in grief, he felt lighter, his mother still with him because of this path she'd put him on. The initial resentment had melted away, replaced by excitement at experiencing the unknown. He thought about finding an astrologer to give him some insights to add to the powerful lessons and messages he received from the tree spirits. He stayed open to the possibility of seeing his natal chart.

The next night, Samuel walked directly to his mother's sycamore. It stood twenty feet tall. He wondered if the hooded figure had hastened the growth. No matter, there it stood, strong and lit with dark purple energy. A wide beam of violet light blasted from the white trunk directly at Samuel, covering him head to toe in his mother's radiant vitality. His head tingled and his heart swelled.

The luminescence turned pale lavender. There stood a holographic Charlotte, smiling at him, wearing a white silk dress that moved with a breeze that Samuel couldn't feel. She was as he remembered her in youth, walking side-by-side and stopping to talk about a tree or a plant. Elated, Samuel reached out to touch her, but the image wavered, and he pulled his hand back.

Charlotte's voice rang out clearly as she began her story.

This was it! Her story, woven with Samuel's story, would unfold tonight. A pile of oversized pillows appeared on the ground. Samuel settled in to hear whatever his mother would reveal.

The Lawyer

Sycamore: The Beauty of Transformation

I, Charlotte Jones, chose to be planted at Willow Ponds Cemetery so my son could understand his heritage and his gifts. I spent many happy days strolling through these woods and getting educated by the tree spirits, and wanted to be a teacher here myself. These enlightening woods would take years to experience each tree, and so it's my hope that you, Samuel, do just that.

It's a rare gift to hear the stories of the trees. I passed this talent down to you, my son. Very few have the power to see the glow of the trees and to retrieve the books and scrolls they hold. It's a secret held within my family. Our heritage includes a line of druids who bought the land where this forest thrives. They felt the magic in the soil and ensured the health of the trees with a volunteer who would forever check on them and use a magic touch to enhance growth. This is the hooded entity you saw. History has lost his name, but his spirit remains powerful.

Samuel, you must not share this ability to read the trees with anyone, otherwise people may seek to cut down the forest for nefarious purposes. The protection of these trees is paramount. There is no replacing them or transplanting the spirits held within them. Their glow radiates around you, and would only do so if they accept you. You can feel good about that. They thrive by sharing their stories with the living. That is your purpose, Samuel. It was my purpose, and now it is yours.

As an attorney, I drew up protective documents to keep these woods as a cemetery for the chosen in perpetuity. The board of directors of Willow Ponds understands the importance of this place. They are the gatekeepers. They allow only wise ones to be planted here. The board of directors of Willow Ponds appoints a special attorney to draw up the wills of those who reside here upon their death. I was the lawyer for us until my demise. Now, I'm happy to be among my friends and to have my son be part of this ancient group.

There are no visitors to this place other than those with the gift. This place only permits one gifted person at a time to visit. That's why I never brought you with me. What I called my *business trips* was when I'd come. That is also why you never see others when you're here. You are currently the only one with gifted perception in the United States. Our lineage has the only bloodline for this work here, so your path includes finding an appropriate mate and having one child with her.

Other cemeteries such as this one exist, with one gifted seer assigned to it, one on each continent. Boards comprising personnel with special gifts find the land and put these cemeteries in place to preserve knowledge, ancient and modern.

That brings me to your father. I met him in a remote village in the rainforest of South America. His name was Mateo Diaz. He was a powerful shaman, able to commune with spirits, travel astrally, and perform healing rituals. Part of his work was connecting with nature, understanding the ultimate reality of the universe, and speaking to plants and trees. We fell in love and spent the months I lived there finding and establishing a *wisdom forest,* as he liked to call it, and creating you. We planted him in the wisdom forest near his village a decade ago. He was much older than me and lived a fulfilling and astonishing life.

As a combination of the two of us, you are more powerful than either of us individually. I left a note for you in my safe deposit box with a map and the names of those in his community who are waiting for you to contact them. I'm sure you'd like to visit your father's tree, but you'd need permission from the gifted one of that forest and must go alone to adhere to the rules. He is a majestic oak tree.

You'll find there are also several suitable wives who are shamans trained by Mateo, but not directly in your father's bloodline. I hope you find love with one of them and bring her back here to build a life and have a child.

You'll have a place on the sacred board to give them updates and recommendations on Willow Ponds and the welfare of this forest. We have warded the entire property with protections to prevent people from cutting down trees. Serious penalties befall those who disrespect the forest.

I know you've searched for your purpose, Samuel. Now you understand why you couldn't know what it is until now. I know I'm leaving Willow Ponds in excellent hands, and one day, I look forward to sharing our story with my granddaughter. I love you.

Samuel's Purpose

Samuel watched his mother gracefully fade into a pinpoint of light. Dumbfounded, he stared at the spot where his mother's spirit was a moment ago. He wished he could have asked questions, like how she knew she'd have a granddaughter and if he could write the stories of the tree spirits without revealing how he got them. Maybe that was a question for the sacred board.

Samuel had only a couple of girlfriends in his thirty-eight years on the planet and now discovered he had a wife waiting for him on another continent. Fear and excitement rippled through him. There were so many adventures awaiting him, so much to look forward to.

With no time to waste, he sped home and made airline reservations for South America. He felt his new wife would like his house. When he brought her home, they would find a dog and have a child. He'd never thought of himself as a family man, but he'd evolved since entering the forest. With a clear vision ready to manifest, he slept soundly, knowing his journey had just begun.

Book Club Discussion Questions

1. What did all the stories/tree spirits have in common?
2. How did Samuel change over the course of his adventure?
3. What was your favorite story? Why?
4. Of all the characters, which natural gift would you want to possess?
5. What is/are your special gift(s)? Are you still searching for it?
6. Which character did you most relate to? Why?
7. What lessons did you get from the stories? Which stories most resonate with you?
8. Which stories did you not relate to?
9. If you were a tree spirit, which story from your life would you share with Samuel?
10. Which story would you like to see expanded?
11. What have you wished for and gotten that you wish you hadn't?
12. Have you ever had your astrology chart read? What insights did you gain?
13. Do you feel connected to nature? Which environments feel strongest to you?
14. Would you want to be buried with a sapling and turn into a tree? What kind of tree would you choose?

15. How would you describe Samuel's journey through the Forest of the Dead?

16. At what point do you think Samuel valued his experience in the forest?

17. Why do you think Samuel's mother never told him about their special relationship to Willow Ponds?

18. Do you think Samuel's mother chose a legal career because of her relationship with Willow Ponds?

19. Do you think the tree symbolism added to the meaning of the story?

20. Who was the hooded figure? Did Samuel fear the hooded figure? What was your reaction to the hooded figure?

21. Why do you think Samuel visited Willow Ponds at dusk and during the evenings? Would you have done that?

22. If you were going to recommend this book to a good friend, how would you describe it?

Don't miss out!

Visit the website below and you can sign up to receive emails whenever Diane Wing publishes a new book. There's no charge and no obligation.

https://books2read.com/r/B-A-MTLEB-YXTAD

BOOKS 2 READ

Connecting independent readers to independent writers.

About the Author

Diane Wing is a multi-published author of dark fantasy fiction, magical realism, cozy mysteries, and enlightening non-fiction. Her work helps people see the magickal, spiritual, loving side of life with a practical edge.

She views the world as beautiful and mysterious, filled with things to learn and experience. The path led her to become a lifetime student of metaphysics, mysticism, magick, and spirituality and to achieve a master's degree in psychology... and it all shows up in her writing. You never know what's waiting around the bend.

Diane is an avid reader and bibliophile with a deep love of trees and animals. She and her husband are doting pet parents to Lily, a Shih Tzu mix, and Chiquita, a Chihuahua.

- Find out more, join her community, listen to Wing Academy Radio, and take the Vibrational Quiz at www.DianeWing.com.

- Check out her author website and join her community to get notified about book discounts and new projects at www.DianeWingAuthor.com.

- Take the Wing Academy Archetype Quiz and take a free class at https://www.dianewing.com/wing-academy/

Read more at https://dianewingauthor.com/.